Sweet MERCY

Sweet Mercy

Empire Nightclub #1

K.A. TUCKER

ISBN 978-1-990105-46-3 (Ingram paperback edition)
ISBN 978-1-990105-00-5 (KDP paperback edition)
ISBN 978-1-9990154-4-2 (ebook edition)

Editing by Hot Tree Editing

Cover design by Shanoff Designs

Published by K.A. Tucker Books Ltd.

Printed in the United States of America

1 MERCY

"Mercy Wheeler!"

My body, already rigid, stiffens at the sound of my name on the guard's tongue. I've been waiting in Fulcort Penitentiary's visitor lounge for over two hours now, long enough to leave me doubting whether I'd ever be let in.

Shutting my textbook, I collect my purse and rush for the counter with my stomach in my throat, afraid that any dallying could lose me my visit with my father.

The guard staff changed over at some point, because the thin older gentleman with the kind smile who took down my information earlier has been replaced by a burly oaf with beady little eyes and an unfriendly face. His name tag reads Parker. "Who you here to see?" he demands in a gruff tone.

"My dad." I clear the wobble from my voice. "Duncan Wheeler. It should say that on the log?" It comes out as a question, though I can see my father's name written in block letters next to the tip of this guy's pen.

"I like to double-check, is all." He smirks, then recites a long string of numbers and letters. My father's inmate ID number. "This is your first visit here?"

"Yeah." My father only began his sentence two weeks ago, and it took time to get me approved on his visitor list, which is bullshit. I'm the *only person* on his visitor list.

Parker the guard takes a long, lingering scan of my plain, baggy T-shirt. That, along with my loosest pair of jeans, is what I carefully chose to comply with the prison's visitor dress code policy. No tank tops, no shorts, no miniskirts. Nothing tight. Nothing to "provoke" the men serving time behind these bars.

His eyes stall on my chest for far too long.

I fight the urge to fidget under the lecherous gaze. He's at least twenty years older than me and unappealing, to say the least. Just imagining what kinds of thoughts are churning in his dirty mind makes my skin crawl. Then again, *everything* in this place—the barbed wire fences, the heavily armed guards, the long and narrow hallways, the constant buzzing as door locks are released, the fact that I'm about to sit in a room with murderers, rapists, and God only knows who else— makes my skin crawl.

"What's your old man in for?" Parker finally asks.

I hesitate. "Murder." Are prison guards supposed to be asking these types of questions?

"Yeah?" His gaze drops to my chest again, and he's not trying to be discreet about it. "And who'd your daddy kill, sweetheart?"

I'm not your goddamn sweetheart. My anger flares, at the

invasion of my privacy, at the term he so casually tosses out, at the lustful stare. "Some asshole who wouldn't take no for an answer from me." A mechanic named Fleet who worked at the same auto repair shop where my dad worked, a slimy guy who smelled of motor oil and weed and apparently jerked off to cut-and-paste photos of my face atop porn mag bodies. Who cornered me one night with the full intention of experiencing the real thing.

My father didn't mean to kill him and yet here he is, serving twenty-two years because of a freak accident. Because the prosecutor was convinced otherwise and decided to make an example of him. Because we hired the world's most ineffective lawyer. It's the first thing I dwell on when my eyelids crack every day and the heaviest thing on my shoulders when I drift off at night.

I'm exhausted by guilt and anger, and it doesn't seem like it's going to let up any time soon.

Pervy Parker smirks. "Lock your things up in number seventeen and then head to security screening." He slaps a key onto the counter with his meaty paw. "Phone, car keys, coins, belt. Don't forget so much as a coin, unless you wanna get strip-searched." His mouth curves into a salacious smile. "And you won't get to say no to that if you ever wanna see your daddy again."

My face twists with horror before I can smother it. They wouldn't *actually* strip-search me for forgetting to take out a penny from my pocket, would they?

The prick laughs. "Welcome to Fulcort Penitentiary."

Who is she here to see? I wonder, watching the shriveled old lady fidget with her knuckles, her hair styled in tight gray curls, her wrinkled features touched with smears of pink and blue makeup. A husband? A son?

I've kept my eyes forward and down since I passed through the airport-level security screening process and was led me to this long, narrow visitation room. I've set my jaw and ignored the hair-raising feel of lingering looks and the stifling tension that courses through the air. My father warned me against attracting attention, that having inmates knowing he has "such a beautiful daughter" would only make his life harder in here. While I rolled my eyes as he said that, I also decided to heed his warning the best way I can, so as not to ruin his life further.

So, no makeup, no styled hair—I didn't even brush it today—and minimal eye contact.

Except this sweet-looking grandmother who sits at the cafeteria-style table across from me has caught my gaze and now I can't help but occupy my mind with questions about her while I wait. Namely, how many Saturdays has she spent sitting at Fulcort waiting for a loved one, and what will *I* look like when I'm sitting in this chair twenty-two *years* from now?

A soft buzz sounds on my left, pulling my attention away from her and toward the door where prisoners have been filtering in and out.

An ache swells in my chest as I watch my father shuffle through. It's only been two weeks and yet his face looks gaunt, the orange jumpsuit loose on his tall, lanky frame.

He pauses as the guard refers to a clipboard, his gaze frantically scanning the faces at each table.

I dare a small wave to grab his attention.

The second his green eyes meet mine, his face splits with a smile. He rushes for me.

"Walk!" a guard barks from somewhere.

I stand to meet him.

"Oh God, are you a sight for sore eyes!" He ropes his arms around my neck and pulls me tight into his body.

"I missed you so much!" I return the embrace, sinking into my father's chest as tears spill down my cheeks despite my best efforts to keep them at bay. "They made me wait for hours. I wasn't sure if I'd make it in today—"

"That's enough!" That same guard who just yelled at my father to walk moves in swiftly to stand beside us, his hard face offering not a shred of sympathy. "Unless you wanna lose visitation privileges, inmate!"

Dad pulls back with a solemn nod, his hands in the air in a sign of surrender. "Sorry." He gestures to the table. "Come on, Mercy. Sit. Let me look at you."

We settle into our seats across from each other, my father folding his hands tidily in front of him atop the table. A model of best behavior. The guard shoots him another warning look before continuing on.

"So?" I swallow against the lump in my throat, brushing my tears away. I've done so well, hiding tears from him up until now. "How are you doing?"

He shrugs. "You know. Fine, I guess." He quickly surveys the occupants of the tables around us.

That's when I notice that his jaw is tinged with a greenish-yellow bruise. "Dad! What happened to your face?" I reach for him on instinct.

He pulls back just as the tips of my fingernails graze his cheek. "It's nothing."

"Bullshit! Did someone hit you?"

His wary eyes dart to the nearby inmates again. "Don't worry about it, Mercy. It's just the way things are inside. Someone thinks you looked at them funny … Pecking order, that sort of thing. It's not hard to make enemies in a prison without trying. Anyway, it's almost healed."

My eyes begin to sting again. This is *my* fault. I should never have told him about what Fleet did that night. It's not like the dirty pig succeeded in his mission; a swift kick to his balls gave me the break I needed to run inside and call the police. Now, had the police done their goddamn job, Fleet never would have strolled into work the next morning with a smug smile on his face and a vivid description of how firm my ass is, and my normally mild-mannered father wouldn't have lost his temper.

Two weeks in and he's already been attacked? My father is one of the most easygoing guys I've ever met. The fact that he went after Fleet the way he did in the garage was a surprise to everyone, including Fleet, according to what witnesses said.

"Hey, hey, hey … Come on. I can't handle watching you cry," my dad croons in a soothing voice. "And we don't have time for that. Tell me what's going on with you. How's school? Work?"

I grit my jaw to keep my emotions in check. We're supposed to have an hour, but the guard already warned me that Saturdays are busy and this visit will most likely get cut short. So much for prisoner rights. "Work is work. Same old." I've been an administrative assistant at a drug and alcohol addiction center called Mary's Way in downtown Phoenix for six years now. The center is geared toward women and children, and there never seems to be a shortage of them passing through our doors, hooked on vodka or heroin or crack. Some come by choice, others are mandated by the court.

Too many suddenly stop coming. Too many times I feel like we're of no help at all.

Dad nods like he knows.

Because he *does* know, thanks to my mother and her own addiction to a slew of deadly drugs. Heroin is the one that claimed her life when I was ten.

"And school? You're keeping up with that, right?"

I hesitate.

"Mercy—"

"*Yes*, I'm still going." Only because it was too late to drop out of my courses without receiving a failing grade. Though, given my scores on my recent midterms, I may earn a failing grade anyway.

He taps the table with his fingertip. "You need to keep up with that, Mercy. Don't let my mess derail your future. You've worked too hard for this, and you're so close to getting that degree."

I've been working toward my bachelor's degree part-time since I was eighteen, squeezing in classes at night and wherever I could find the time and money. At twenty-five, I'm two passing grades away from achieving it. Up until now my intention has always been to become a substance abuse counselor, to help other families avoid the same anguish and loss that my father and I live with. That's why I took the job at Mary's to begin with.

But shit happened, and now I have another focus, and it is laser-specific.

I swallow. "I'm looking at taking the LSAT."

"LSAT?" My dad frowns. "That have something to do with being a counselor?" My father isn't a highly educated man. He spent his teenage years working on cars and skipping class to get high. At some point he decided school wasn't for him, so he wrote his GED and then got a job in a mechanic shop. It took years, but he finally got licensed.

"No. It's for getting into law school." I level him with a serious gaze. "If you'd had a better lawyer than that shyster, you would have gotten involuntary manslaughter at most. Your sentence would have been a sliver of what you're facing now—"

"No, wait." He pinches the bridge of his nose. "What are you saying, Mercy? That you're going to give up on your plans and go to law school just so you can try and get me out of here? I mean, do you even wanna be a lawyer? I thought you hated lawyers." He chuckles as if the idea is amusing.

Nothing is amusing about this. "I want to be able to hug you without some guard breathing down our necks." My voice has turned hoarse. "I want my kids to be able to play and laugh with their grandfather." It's going to be years before there are actually tiny feet running about. But will my fifty-year-old father live long enough to see the outside again?

"I don't like this at all." Dad shakes his head. "How many years of school is it, anyway?"

"A lot less than what you have to serve right now." Three full-time, plus articling. If I get accepted anywhere. I've always exceled in my courses, but this is a new direction, one I've never spent a second considering. And then there's the whole "how do I pay for tuition and survive for three years while I'm going to law school full-time" question. All of our savings went to that joke of a lawyer who screwed my father.

It's a lot to figure out, but I *will* figure it out, because there is no way I'll accept coming here every Saturday for the next twenty-two years to watch my father wither away.

"This isn't the life I hoped for you. But I know better than to argue with you." Dad sighs, his shoulders sinking. "So … what's the weather like? I haven't been outside yet today."

"Sunny. Hot."

"Shocking." He offers me a wry smile.

Despite my mood, I can't help but chuckle. It's always one or the other in the desert. A lot of the time, it's both, and in July, it's oppressively so. But the eternal sunshine is the main reason we moved to Arizona from North Carolina after my mother died. It's a natural mood-booster, my father says, and he has always worried about me inheriting her depression. "I had to change in the parking lot." The dented blue shitbox that I drive has never had working air-conditioning, so I pulled my T-shirt and jeans on over my shorts and tank top. "Figure I'll leave these clothes in the car for Saturdays. It'll be like my prison uniform."

He makes a sound. "Good call. Maybe bring a paper bag to wear over your head too."

"*Dad.*"

"Trust me, I've heard the way the men in here talk about women, especially pretty young women like you." His eyes narrow on a guy three tables over whose dark eyes flitter curiously to us—to me—while a ready-to-burst pregnant woman sitting across from him babbles away. "I don't want anyone giving you grief when you come visit me."

"Nobody is going to give me grief." Except that guard, Parker, but there's no way I'm telling my dad about him. "And if anyone says anything, *ignore* it. They're just words."

He harrumphs. "How's the new place?"

I avert my gaze, dragging my fingertip across the table in tiny circles. "Fine."

He sighs. "That bad?"

"It's lacking charm," I admit. Anyone who has lived in Phoenix for long enough knows which areas of the city to avoid, and when my dad's conviction was passed and we accepted the fact that I'd need to downgrade from the two-bedroom apartment we were sharing—a downgrade from the house we had before that—we started looking for cheap one-bedrooms closer to work and campus. We found one. A relatively clean, quiet twelve-unit complex with decent management and minimal needles littering the parking lot. A diamond in the rough, my dad called it.

Turns out it's more like a diamond in Mordor.

The couple two doors down—Bob and Rita—fight like they're sworn enemies. I've watched her launch glass from their fourth-storey balcony, aiming for his head as he runs to his car. The cops have been there twice that I know of. It's only a matter of time before an ambulance is wheeling someone out—my bet is it's Bob.

And then there's my next-door-neighbor, Glen, a hairy-chested guy who I hear every morning through the thin walls masturbating to the tune of my 7:00 a.m. alarm and who likes to knock on my door in the middle of the night, bleary-eyed and wearing nothing but his boxers. He always asks for Doritos. I tell him I don't buy Doritos—I *hate* Doritos—but he keeps coming back. I'm beginning to think Doritos is code for something else.

I don't open the door for him anymore.

And I'm not telling my father any of this. He has enough to worry about in here.

The guards come around, tapping several inmates on the shoulder to let them know that their time is up. That earns countless pained expressions from both prisoners and visitors alike. My dad and I watch as people embrace, some adhering to the rules while others hold on until they get a bark of warning.

That'll be us before long, and then it'll be another week before I make the hourlong drive up here.

My heart sinks. "What's your cellmate like?"

Dad smirks. "His name is Crazy Bob. And yes, they call him Crazy Bob to his face. Haven't asked what he's in for, and I don't think I wanna know. He likes the violin and NASCAR. Hasn't tried to shank or rape me in my sleep yet."

I frown my disapproval for the poor joke. "The violin and NASCAR. That's an odd combination, right?"

"Yeah. You could say that," my dad agrees. "But Crazy Bob is odd. He seems all right so far. Been in here over ten years now. Knows everything about everything. He's been giving me the lay of the land, so to speak. Where the minefields are, so I can avoid 'em."

"That's good. And the food?"

"The peas are mushy, the potatoes are grainy, and I've fixed tires that had more give than the meat they served last night." He chuckles. "So, kind of like your cooking. In fact, did you take a job in the kitchen that I don't know about?"

"Har. Har. Har." Leave it to my dad to try to make jokes in terrible circumstances. But he's always had a natural ability to defuse any tense situation.

So how did he end up getting punched in the face?

I bite the inside of my cheek, wondering if I should push. Finally, I can't help it. "Dad, why did someone hit you?"

He waves it off. "Aww ... it was nothing—"

"So then tell me about it, if it's nothing," I challenge, wielding that sharp edge in my voice that Dad swears is like listening to a recording of my mother.

The longer he studies the smooth surface of the

table, the more I'm convinced that my gut is right and it's not just a matter of a pissing contest or a funny look.

"Dad ..."

"Apparently Fleet's got family or something in here. He wanted me to know he wasn't happy with what happened to Fleet, is all." Dad shrugs nonchalantly. "So now I know. I'm just gonna stay out of the guy's way and everything'll be fine." His jaw tenses. He's more worried about it than he's letting on.

Rightfully so. My father is locked up in here with a family member of the guy he killed and he's already attacked him.

I think I'm going to vomit.

"We need to tell the guards—"

"No." He shakes his head firmly. "Trust me, *no*, Mercy. That won't do me *any* good in a place like *this*. Fulcort's known for ... Well, let's just say I'm a guy with no friends, no affiliations. I'm best to fly under the radar."

I frown. "What do you mean, affiliations?"

His gaze drifts around the room. I follow it, taking in the various men in orange jumpsuits. The population of Fulcort penitentiary is made up of every age and skin tone—short, tall, fat, skinny, clean-faced, scruffy.

How many of these men are like my father, I wonder.

How many of them don't belong in here?

Probably a lot less than the number of men who earned their cell.

My dad drops his voice. "You see that guy over

there? With the tattoo on his face? Don't be too obvious."

I shift my gaze to my left, spotting the guy in question easily. Half his face is marred with ink—a scaly dragon with talons—making him look downright scary. He's sitting across from a young pretty Latina girl with fake nails long enough to be used as a weapon in a place like this, I'd hazard. "Yeah."

"Crazy Bob says he's high up in some notorious LA gang. Anything that guy wants in here, he gets. Anything."

"So become his friend."

Dad chuckles. "That's not how it works." He glances over his shoulder at the group of inmates filtering in. "See that one there? The third in line?"

I watch a heavyset man with pock-marked cheeks and unkempt gray hair stroll in. He must be in his seventies, with a belly that strains the waistline of his prison garb. "Okay."

"He's got the warden and plenty of the guards in his pocket. Even dragon-face stays away from him. He could put a hit out on anyone and it'd be done in a day, inside these walls or not. That's what Crazy Bob claims, anyway."

I watch the man lumber along. Maybe it's the jumpsuit and shaggy mop on his head but I'm picturing him stretching pizza dough or selling car insurance from behind a chunky old desk circa 1970, not swimming at the top of the food chain in a maximum security prison, scaring LA gangbangers.

"What's his deal?"

"Mob boss. Big into the drug trade."

I feel my eyebrows pop. "As in, like, Al Capone?"

"As in, you betray him, he takes out your entire family first and then you, and then he pisses on your ashes." Dad's voice drops to a whisper. "Crazy Bob told me that some clueless do-gooder guard came in here last year, stirring the pot against the corruption. He didn't last long."

"As in fired?"

"As in stopped coming in. His family hasn't heard from him since." Dad gives me a knowing look.

"I feel so much better knowing you're spending your days with these kind of people," I mutter, nausea stirring in my stomach. I study the mob boss as he passes. He walks with ease, as if he owns this room and he knows it. And maybe Crazy Bob isn't blowing smoke. Maybe he does own this place.

Curious about who he's here to see—one of his mobster minions, probably?—I let my gaze follow him to the four-person table in the far corner.

And find myself suddenly ensnared in a storm.

2 GABRIEL

I WAS PREPARED for two things when my eyelids peeled open this morning: one, that I'd be nursing a fucking epic hangover for most of the day after last night's festivities, and two, that I'd be in an extra-pissy mood by the time I made it up to this shithole.

What I did not expect was to be sitting in Fulcort with a raging hard-on for some chick visiting her old man.

But there you have it.

Fuck.

I've been coming here once a month for the last three years to see my father and I have *never* laid eyes on that woman before. I'd remember. Those sharp cheekbones, that thick jet-black hair. Those fat fucking lips, the kind that were made for wrapping around my cock and sucking slowly. She's hiding her body in baggy clothes—standard protocol, though she's taken it to the extreme; she's one step away from men's sweatpants—but her arms are toned, her neck is slender and long, her olive skin looks silky soft. I'm a betting man and I'd bet there's a tight ass and tits that sway when she's riding hard hiding beneath all that.

I didn't notice her at first. I came in, settled into my dad's usual table in the corner of the room, and started surveying all the degenerates filling the room on this fine Saturday afternoon, killing time until Dad decided to grace me with his presence.

And then I spotted her over there, her pretty brow furrowed in worry as she leaned over the table to get as close to the man as possible without setting off the guards, and I haven't been able to peel my gaze away since.

It's been forever and a day since a woman has stirred my blood like this.

What's even more interesting is that she and the guy she's visiting—her dad, maybe?—leaned in to share a few whispered words and then those big, brown eyes of hers shifted to the inmates coming in.

To my father.

With wariness, she watched him stroll all the way over, and that's how, bingo, we're now eye-fucking each other. At least, that's what *I'm* doing.

Until I can get out of here, track her down, and switch to straight-up fucking.

My dad settles his girth into the stiff chair across from me. Somehow he's managed to pack on fifty pounds eating shitty prison food peppered with the odd steak dinner. "You're late," he mutters in his typical gruff voice.

"You have somewhere else you need to be?" I throw

back before I can bite my tongue. If he wasn't going to complain about that, it'd be about something else. Still, he doesn't take too kindly to attitude, and Dad's bad side is not one you ever want to be on, blood-related or not. "Got caught up with work," I lie. "Who's that new guy over there? Number seven." I nod toward the table.

"What do I look like? Fucking four-one-one?" he snaps back, irritated.

I shrug, acting all nonchalant. "He seemed interested in you when you came in, is all."

Dad's bushy eyebrows furrow with the glare he shoots me before peering over his shoulder. "New fish. A nobody," he declares.

It's at that precise moment that my future lay glances our way. Her chocolate-brown eyes flare and then snap back, her face paling. Yeah, I'd say she got the skinny on who my father is, and it scares her. But will she be scared of me too? If so, what can I do to ease her fears?

My dick twitches with eagerness.

Dad shakes his head. "How's the club doing? You and Caleb haven't run it into the ground yet?"

"It's running smooth." Better than smooth, and he knows it. He likes to talk about Empire like it's his club, like it was his idea in the first place. He had nothing to do with it. My older brother and I purchased an old factory warehouse and converted it into a nightclub eight years ago. It's gone through several identity transformations but it's found its stride, catering to high-end clientele with cash to burn and people to impress. A one hundred percent legitimately run business, as far as any law enforcement is concerned. And, trust me, they've tried to prove otherwise. That's the downside of being the sons of Vlad Easton: you have the Feds and the IRS crawling up your ass on the regular.

"Peter was here last week." His cold gray eyes watch me. "He said our *friends* have been causing problems for Harriet again."

By friends, Dad means the cartel, aka nobody's friend, and by causing problems for Harriet, he means venturing farther into US territory and encroaching on my family's foothold in the lucrative cocaine and heroin trade. It's a business that my father and his brother, Peter, have been nurturing for decades, originating with a supply arrangement from "our friends" down south.

A business that has amassed us impressive wealth and power.

"So what's Peter going to do?" My uncle is a crazy fuck—almost as crazy as my dad, who isn't quite as crazy as the cartel.

His sagging skin contorts with his sneer. "What's *he* going to do? How about what are my sons going to do!" He stabs at the table's surface with his meaty index finger. "It's time you two stop fucking around like a bunch of playboys and act like you're ready to take care of the family business."

I bite my tongue against the urge to remind him that we've laundered millions through Empire for "the family business," and that it's Caleb and me who keep the highly lucrative underground fight ring going. We can't talk openly about it here, and besides, he doesn't want to hear that. He definitely doesn't want to hear the thoughts Caleb floated after the handcuffs landed on

Dad's wrists almost four years ago—that it's time to let the cartel move in, wash our hands of the dirty drug business, and invest all this money in other, legitimate things. Things that won't land us in this shithole with him.

But it's like Dad reads my mind. "What do you think, that you two could afford any of your cars and your houses and your club if not for all the sacrifices your uncle and I have made? All the blood and sweat that's poured. The tears?"

I highly doubt any of those tears came from my father. He didn't even cry when my mother died. The guy's tear ducts probably don't work. And I damn well know none of that pouring blood was his, though there's been more than enough spilled thanks to "Harriet."

He's right though: we've gotten filthy rich off junkies shooting their veins with heroin and partiers filling their nostrils with cocaine.

I sigh reluctantly. "We'll go talk to Peter."

"Good. Because I want things running smoothly for when I get out."

You're not getting out of here. Dad's pushing seventy-five—he was in his midforties when Caleb and I were born—and he has another six years to serve for the witness tampering and money laundering convictions the Feds nailed him on. A drop in the bucket compared to what they *could* put him away for, if they could find their assholes in the dark.

Harriet alone would put him away for life three times over. Could put *all* of us away, something my brother and I are not so keen on risking. Sure, when we were younger, we felt invincible. But Caleb's thirty-one, I'm twenty-nine, and I'm looking at the indomitable Vlad Easton in an orange jumpsuit, sitting in a place where he swore he would never end up. And my brother and I? We've done the math. A lifetime behind these walls isn't worth it, not when we're already living like royalty.

I'd say we've been smart, for the most part, keeping our hands relatively clean. Or looking clean, at least. That was always the strategy. But what Dad's demanding now is the opposite of keeping our hands clean. He's telling us to sink our hands deep into Harriet's dirty, disease-riddled cunt.

No fucking thank you.

And then there's the matter of dealing with the goddamn cartel. I wouldn't say I'm *afraid* of them—we have our own network of proficient "fixers" to deal with threats, and I've learned to hold my own. I would just rather not wake up one morning to my head separated from my body.

Caleb and I have discussed the future of the Easton empire already. Neither of us trust Dad's judgment anymore. He and Uncle Peter are old-school, where giving your word is an iron-clad agreement and going against it earns you a brutal punishment; where R-E-S-P-E-C-T isn't just a catchy song, it's a way of life. They put way too much stock in the belief that blood breeds loyalty.

Caleb and me? We live by one rule: don't trust *anyone* but each other.

That's where Dad made his mistake, bringing

Marek, some third cousin born to a whore back in Russia, into the fold. Dear cousin Marek is now feeding worms in an undisclosed location, but before he ended up there, he gave the Feds just enough of a smoking gun to tuck my father away for almost a decade.

A guard passes through, stalling at table seven. The crestfallen look on my raven beauty's face tells me that her visit is over. *Shit.* If I can duck out of here early and cut her off in the parking lot, I could earn myself a blow job before the drive home—

"We need to go over some things," my dad says, slipping a wad of paper out from somewhere unseen and sliding it across the table to me. Prisoners aren't allowed to bring anything in with them, but the guards look the other way when it's us.

I unfold it to reveal a full eight-and-a-half by eleven sheet covered in encrypted codes that only Caleb and I and our accountant can decipher to hidden overseas accounts that the Feds didn't manage to turn up in their investigation.

This is going to take forever.

I sigh heavily as I watch the woman wrap her arms around the man's neck and squeeze tight, tears running down her cheeks. Her father, I'm guessing. Or uncle. Family. Definitely not her husband.

The guy's shoulders sink as he's led back to the cells with her watching him the entire way.

Not until he's out of sight does she move for the visitor entrance, her gaze drifting over mine in a slow pass. It's only for a second or two, just long enough for me to note the way her lips part, the way her dark eyes skitter over my chest and arms, the way her cheeks flush, and then she swallows hard, ducks her head, and walks stiffly and quickly for the exit, those baggy jeans doing nothing for the tight ass I'm imagining.

"Gabriel!" my father barks, spearing me with a glare. "Chase pussy on your own time."

I plan on it.

———

"Parker. Hey." I rest my elbows on the security desk.

The sweaty, overweight guard leans back in his chair. "Gabriel Easton … what can I do for you today?"

I've never liked this dumb fuck, but I tolerate him because he's as pliable as putty. He's also worse than a twelve-year-old girl when it comes to spreading gossip, but he knows better than to chirp about me. "There was a woman in here, visiting an inmate. She left a half hour ago. About five eight, long black hair and—"

"Say no more." A shit-eating grin stretches his ugly mug. "Damn, that was a fine piece of ass. At least, I'm guessing. Sounds like she's coming back next Saturday. I'm gonna get her into a room to find out what's under—"

"Yeah, yeah." As if he'd be conducting a strip search himself. They have female staff for that. But he's already given me one vital piece of information—she'll be back next week. "What do you know about her?"

"Why do ya wanna know?"

I level him with a severe look.

It has the desired effect. "Let's see. Her name is …"

Parker lifts a page on his clipboard. "Oh right, how could I forget? *Mercy* Wheeler. As in 'have mercy on my soul.' And my dick." He lets out a loud snort-laugh.

I ignore his idiocy, unable to stop the smile that slowly stretches across my lips.

Mercy.

My sweet, sweet Mercy.

You will be mine.

3 MERCY

THE FIRST TIME I walked through the flimsy door of Mary's Way, I was twelve years old. I came for a group therapy session geared toward teenagers struggling with their parents' drug addiction.

I hadn't been struggling anymore. My mother was already dead.

But I was angry—at her for letting herself fall victim, at myself for not being enough to keep her here—and so my dad thought maybe I'd be able to get comfort and answers this way. It couldn't hurt, after all. And it was free.

Marsha Thompson was the counselor—a loud, curvy woman with hair cropped close to her scalp, eyebrows that seemed to have a life of their own with all their arching and curling, and a severe voice that made you think you were about to get in trouble for something you did.

She somehow said all the things I needed to hear that day. I walked out of Mary's sure of two things: that what happened to my mother had nothing to do with me and that I wanted to be Marsha Thompson when I grew up.

I kept coming back to the addiction center, volunteering after school and, when I was older, in between working shifts at a local restaurant. And then one day when I was nineteen, Marsha, who had been appointed Director at Mary's Way, offered me an administrative job. A shit-paying job with a lot of grunt work, she warned, but a chance to slowly familiarize myself with the world of drug addiction counselors and gain invaluable experience while I earned courses toward my degree.

She lamented that she wouldn't ever be able to give me a raise on account of the sad state of her publicly funded budget—she couldn't even afford basic building repairs on this dilapidated space—but what she *could* give me is the private, tiny cubicle tucked away in the back, perfect for plugging away without being disturbed.

This cubicle has become a comfort zone to me, especially with the upheaval in my life. The high walls make it feel almost like my own private office.

Almost.

The downside is that I don't get a lot of warning when someone's coming.

"You put in the supplies order yet?" Marsha's stern voice arrives a second before she appears beside me, making me jump. She chuckles, because for some reason she gets a kick out of startling me like that. "I'm sorry."

"It's okay. And I haven't. I have it finished." I gesture at the order form on my computer monitor. All the computers at Mary's are from the dinosaur age, but we can't afford to upgrade. Big surprise. "*But* the bill to fix the staff toilet is five hundred bucks, so … how badly do we need printer ink, do you think?" Part of my job is helping manage our monthly operations budget. I do a pretty good job, but I can't make wine from water. I'm not Jesus.

She shakes her head. "Leaky roof last month, broken fridge the month before. This place is falling apart on us. How can they expect us to work under these conditions?"

"And maybe I can find a cheaper brand of coffee?" We keep a brewed pot going at all times. People fighting the urge to get high or drunk can't also deal with caffeine withdrawal. Neither can the underpaid, over-worked counselors.

Marsha peers over her glasses at me, and the look she gives me is severe. "We're already drinking swamp water out there, Mercy."

I shrug. "Bring your own cream?"

She sighs heavily. "Do what you have to. Except for the printer ink. We need that. Just send a memo out to the staff. Draft quality printing and digital where we can. *No* personal printing of *any* kind."

"Got it." I avert my gaze. Has she figured out that I've been printing out my class assignments here?

"You look tired, hon. You okay?"

"Yeah, I'm fine. I just didn't sleep well this week-end." It's been months since I've slept through the night. I caved and filled a prescription for Ambien that my doctor insisted I consider, but I still haven't cracked the bottle, too afraid that one occasional pill will turn into a nightly requirement, which will turn into me wandering the streets for my next heroin high. That may be a tad drastic, but when your own mother had addiction problems and you're living in the lowest point of your life right now since she died, bad things can happen.

"You went to see your father this weekend?" Marsha's voice is softer, more quiet.

I nod, that constant knot in my throat swelling.

"How's he doing?"

"Not good." I tell her about Fleet's vengeful family member. Marsha is intimately aware of all the details surrounding the case. It was outside in Mary's parking lot that Fleet attacked me. My engine wouldn't turn, so I called my dad, who called his boss, Billy, who sent Fleet over with the tow truck.

Marsha—and everyone here at Mary's—has been by my side for the horror that unfolded since that fateful night.

She gives my shoulder a comforting pat. "Have you filed the appeal yet?"

"Not yet. I need to find a new lawyer." A reputable one, not like that shyster. And I need money.

I need a lot of things.

"Okay, well, just know, I'm prayin' for the both of you."

"Thanks." I offer her what I hope is an appreciative smile. She does that—prays a lot. It hasn't helped us one lick so far.

Marsha heads off, leaving me to stare blankly at the

spreadsheet that I've been playing dollar Jenga with all morning, to no avail.

I decide that it's time for my morning break. Peeking over my cubicle to make sure there's no one around, I do something I've been wondering about since Saturday. I open up the internet search browser and type in Crime Boss Phoenix Arizona Prison Fulcort Drugs. One of those words has to lead somewhere.

I click on Go. Twenty matches appear on the screen. I don't end up going through them all because the first one gives me what I want.

Vladimir Easton, convicted of money laundering and witness tampering in a drug case three years ago. It's definitely the same man I saw at Fulcort. The article includes a courtroom picture. He was thinner back then, and wearing a sharp-looking suit. But his cold, dead eyes are a match to the ones I met. I almost pissed my pants when I glanced over to find him turned in his seat and giving my father and me the once-over. The last thing I ever want is to be on that guy's radar. It's bad enough that I seem to have caught the attention of his visitor, a guy in his late twenties with eyes as dark and moody as a storm rolling in and a chiseled jaw that could have been carved out of stone. Hell, all of him could have been carved from stone from what I could see, his gray T-shirt hugging brawny arms and stretched over a padded chest. The only soft thing about him was his full, plump lips and a stylish mane of thick, sandy brown hair.

Nobody has any business being that damn hot, but especially not a man in league with a crime family boss.

He stole my breath the first time our eyes met. It

wasn't two casual, fleeting glances that crossed paths. No, it was clear he had been watching me for a while. The intensity of that gaze made my stomach drop, even as flutters stirred.

And that look he gave me as I was leaving? I've seen that look before. In the eyes of guys I've dated, moments away from sliding into bed. At clubs, when a man offers to buy me a drink; in my psych class, when my sleazy professor asked me to stay after class to discuss an essay; in Fleet's gaze every time I stopped by Billy's garage.

That look of pure lust.

That beautiful man was lusting for me, and he made no effort to hide it.

Under any other circumstances, I might have been flattered. I might have fallen under his spell. If he'd approached me, I might have gone anywhere with him and given him *anything* he asked for, even though the "I'm not that kind of girl" adage is actually the case with me.

A tremor flows through my body at the idea of having that guy's hands on my body.

But who *is* he? More importantly, who is he to Vladimir Easton? And is he tied up in the same sort of activities?

I type in that name and Google spits out whole dozens of news matches, the top results all about the man in question. As I scan them, my wariness only grows.

That witness tampering charge? The witness mysteriously vanished. They didn't have enough evidence to charge Vladimir Easton with murdering him. And then there was the time nineteen years ago when Vlad Easton was charged with the brutal murder of a man. It was based on circumstantial evidence, the prosecutor claiming it was a retaliatory kill. He was acquitted. No body, no proof.

I keep mining information. There's one particularly scathing opinion piece written not long after that acquittal about how every law official in Arizona and the surrounding states knows that Vlad Easton is a murderer, that the Easton family's obscene wealth comes from decades of illicit activities—drug trafficking, extortion—but no one seems to be smart enough to prove it.

I get lost down a rabbit hole of Vlad Easton's dirty deeds for long enough to be sure that I need to stay as far the hell away from anyone remotely associated with him.

Including the insanely fuckable visitor.

I CHECK my watch for the hundredth time.

11:40 a.m.

That's three hours and ten minutes of sitting in this bland, uncomfortable waiting room, though I made sure to arrive at eight thirty sharp this time, when visiting hours opened.

If there's one thing I can say about Fulcort, it's that it's quickly becoming as predictable as a thief browsing a shop full of jewels.

And, *I swear*, that woman who just passed into security arrived well after me. So did the last five people they called. But I don't dare complain. That leering, strip-search-threatening security guard from last weekend is there again today, stealing frequent looks my way that make the hairs on my arms stand on end.

With a heavy sigh, I sink back into the LSAT prep text book I borrowed from a friend, keeping one ear perked for my name to be called. It's hard to focus—what with all the buzzers buzzing and people milling impatiently and Pervy Parker's brusque barking—but time is not a luxury I can afford to waste, not if I'm actually going to pay the registration fees and take this exam in the fall.

In my periphery, I sense a figure approaching, and a moment later they settle into the chair directly beside me. Even though there's an open section across from me that would give this person—this male, based on the black Adidas and dark wash jeans that I can see from my hunched angle and the spicy cologne I just inhaled—an empty seat on either side of him. But, no, he has to sit down *right beside me*.

I grit my teeth, annoyed. But I'm in a prison waiting area and likely to go in soon, so there's no need to cause a potential scene by getting up and moving. Either way, I shift my body to give him the back of my shoulder.

"You want to be a lawyer, huh?" the stranger says, and somehow his deep, raspy voice slides down my spine like liquid honey.

And now he's reading over my shoulder.

As much as I'd like to ignore him, my father's words from last weekend about making enemies ring in my ear.

I don't need to be making enemies around here either. "Yup," I murmur politely, but keep my head down.

"Smart *and* beautiful. I haven't had that combination. Yet." There's no mistaking the humor in his voice. Or the insinuation.

Had?

Yet?

This is where my politeness ends. "Look, no offense? But I'm not here to get hit on by …" The rest of the words fall off as I turn to find myself caught in intense blue eyes the color of nightfall.

Oh shit.

It's the guy from last week. The sexy-as-all-hell guy.

The one visiting the mob boss.

I clear my throat several times as a wild rash of flutters stirs in my stomach.

His lips curve into a knowing smirk, as if he can sense my reaction. He's somehow even more attractive today. Almost model-pretty, with that cutting jawline, high cheekbones, and deep-set eyes. But the thin layer of stubble coating his cheeks, the rough hands, the slouchy, legs-spread way he sits in that chair radiates masculinity.

Pretty, but likely dangerous, I remind myself. God only knows *how* dangerous. This guy was visiting Fulcort's version of Al Capone last week. For all I know, he's a mob henchman. Maybe he knows where that missing witness went.

Maybe he's the one who helped make him disappear.

I need to stay *far away* from this man.

"I'm no expert, but I'm guessing lawyers who can't

find their tongues don't do well in that profession." His gaze drops to my mouth, where it sits for several beats. "Sorry, what were you saying? Something about not being here to get hit on by …?"

I clear my throat again. Being outright rude to him would be as stupid as welcoming his cocky version of flirtation. I settle for polite honesty. "By *anyone*." But especially not by the goddamn mob.

"I guess it's a good thing I wasn't hitting on you then." His dark blue eyes drift around the room. "You're not my type."

"Well … good." I duck my head as I try to shake my embarrassment. What *is* his type, I wonder? Silicone-filled, no doubt. Likely also dubious morals and a loose—

"Who are you visiting?"

"My father," I find myself answering before I can stop myself. I hesitate. "You?"

He smirks. "Same."

My stomach drops. This guy isn't a mobster minion. He's the *son* of a mob *boss*. Is that better or worse?

"Mercy Wheeler!" Pervy Parker booms.

"Have a nice visit," I mutter, collecting my things and rushing to get away as quickly as possible.

Parker's slimy grin is already firmly in place when I reach the desk.

I hug my textbook to my chest this time, staving off his leering for a few moments at least. "I'm Mercy Wheeler."

"Mercy … Mercy … Mercy … Hey, that'd make one hell of a stage name. Is that your stage name?"

"No." I struggle to keep my eyes from rolling. And it's far from the first time I've been asked that idiotic question. Clearly my parents didn't think the name through when they chose it.

"Too bad. I know a lot of guys who'd drop serious dough to watch you strip. Speaking of stripping—"

"Let her through, Parker," a raspy male voice warns, just inches behind me.

Startling me. I step away as I glance over my shoulder to find that Mob Boss Junior has followed me up to the desk and is now looming over me, leveling those ominous eyes on the guard. He's tall. Well over six feet.

"Gabriel Easton ..." Parker studies him a long moment, his lips twisting with displeasure, as if deciding whether he should say what's on his mind, flex his authority as a prison guard.

His name is Gabriel. An angel's name. Though something tells me there's nothing angelic about this guy.

I suspect that, while Parker may be a lout, he's aware of who Gabriel Easton is and that flexing any kind of muscle would be a bad idea.

I suspect right. He shifts his attention back to me and, slapping a locker key on the counter and jerking his chin toward the security gate, he mutters, "Go on."

Criminal or angel, *Gabriel* just came to my rescue.

Taking a deep breath, I turn to offer him a quick, polite nod of thanks before hightailing it through.

4 GABRIEL

PARKER SPINS in his desk chair and watches Mercy Wheeler rush to the bank of lockers.

"So, what are we playing at here? Good cop, bad cop?"

"We're not playing at anything." *You dumb fuck.* I swear, the guy's brain is the size of a walnut. A shrunken, shriveled walnut buried in the ground in the dead of winter.

He frowns at me like *I'm* the idiot. "Then why'd you make me hold her here so long? She showed up as soon as the doors opened. I've been sittin' here with a semi for the past three hours, looking at her."

A flicker of guilt stirs in me, but I push it aside—it gave her time to study—and shrug. "'Cause I had a late night. Didn't get up before ten." And then I had to rid myself of my "guests"—the two naked blonds I found in my bed when I got home from the club. A "gift" from my brother, who said I looked stressed. Sometimes living

36

with Caleb has its disadvantages—namely the steady stream of scantily clad women he invites into our house at all hours of the day and night.

Not that I'm complaining. I'm just getting so fucking bored of them—they're all the same, no challenge—which is probably I'm here today.

"Yeah, I'll bet." Parker chuckles, like he can guess what my night entailed. "Well, our girl's day is about to turn a whole lot worse."

My little gossip is in the know, as usual.

"Yeah?" I rest my elbows on the counter. "Why is that?"

"Her old man already has an enemy in here."

I watch as Mercy yanks her belt through the loops of her jeans, flashing a second's worth of taut belly skin and a narrow waist. *Damn.* I'm betting those tits of hers are nice. And real. When was the last time I had my hands on real tits? Definitely not last night.

She was nervous when I sat down next to her, when she was about to give me the brush-off before she looked over and saw who I was. But her demeanor didn't shift much after that, and she bolted the second her name was called, as if she couldn't wait to get away from me.

Does she prefer pussy to cock? Is that the issue?

No … not with the fuck-me-eyes she was casting last weekend. I'm not blowing smoke up my own ass either; I'm not some sick bastard who misreads female cues. I know when a woman is attracted to me—all the straight ones are—and Mercy is *definitely* attracted to me.

So my guess is she decided she doesn't want to be. And that likely has to do with knowing who I am. Or rather, who my father is.

That prospect, I don't like.

I'm my own man. I'm no saint, but I'm sure as hell not Vlad Easton.

She secures her locker, and then, throwing a fleeting glance over her shoulder, just long enough to catch me staring at her, she disappears into the security screening, her cheeks flushed. Oblivious to what she's walking into.

"Who's the enemy?" All I know about her father is what Parker told me last week—that he's doing time for offing a guy. But a girl like Mercy, aiming to be a lawyer, doesn't rush to her lowlife murdering father every weekend. Something tells me there's a lot more to that story.

"Diego Montoya."

"Doesn't ring any bells." Not that I know every degenerate behind these bars, but it means he's not a key player.

"One of Puff's guys. A piece of shit. Repeat offender, in for the long haul now."

Well now, *that* is interesting. Puff *is* a key player. An extra-salty fuck with a giant scaly dragon tattoo covering half his face to counter his fluffy street name. I don't know how he ended up being called Puff, but the few people stupid enough to mock him to his ugly face about it didn't find it too funny once they were lying broken on the pavement. That's what landed him in here. He's serving time for beating a guy to near-death outside a club. The whole thing was caught on video. Kind of hard to avoid jail in that case.

"What'd her dad do to piss this Diego guy off?"

"He's family of the guy Mercy's old man whacked, so … he's got a legitimate beef. Second time he's gone after him."

"Hmm." And likely not the last, the way things work here. What else do they have to do, besides wait to corner some poor shit in the yard or the shower? It's a sport. A game of cat and mouse, until the cat gets bored and bites the mouse's head off.

Sounds like Mercy's father will need protection if he doesn't want to lose his head in here. That's something only a few people can give her.

One of those people being me.

I smile to myself as a wicked thought stirs my brain —and my cock. What would Mercy be willing to do for my help in saving dear old Daddy?

Though, this could get tricky.

Puff's gang has been moving merchandise for our family for years, which makes us business partners to a degree. We have a healthy albeit strained level of respect for each other. My father and Uncle Pete value their street-level network, and Puff appreciates that the Easton family has details on the location of every key family member—Puff's elderly mother, his sisters, his barely legal baby mama—that they'll put into play should Puff or any of his guys betray us.

I wonder if Puff knows about this little tiff between his guy and Mercy's father. If he sanctioned it, that could prove complicated for me.

Parker sighs. "So, you want me to send your dad up, or what?"

"Nah." Seeing him once a month is enough for me, and I don't have anything to say that he wants to hear. Caleb and I went to Uncle Peter's house on Wednesday to talk because I said we would. We figured it didn't hurt to find out exactly what happened and offer some suggestions. Mainly, we went to be able to say we went.

Uncle Peter wasn't too welcoming and he sure didn't seem too keen on my father trying to run things from inside Fulcort. "Interfering" was the word he used.

It makes me wonder if, with my father out of the picture, my uncle and cousins are going to angle for a bigger piece of the Easton pie. As in, the whole thing.

"Well then, what'd you do, come all the way up here just for this twisted little game?" Again with that "you're an idiot" frown.

"Fuck no." I snort. Though, if I'm being totally honest, knowing Mercy was going to be here was a big motivating factor. I'll never admit that out loud. That would make me a fucking pussy.

I'm no pussy.

I *want* pussy.

Hers, specifically.

I've been thinking about it all week. Is it bald or groomed? Tight or loose? How many men has she let inside it?

What does she taste like?

I'm desperate to find out.

"Get me Chops," I demand.

"Fine." He reaches for his radio.

"At my table. And get him in there ASAP. I don't wanna waste my day in this sewer system."

Parker sighs with reluctance. "Yeah, sure, no problem."

5 MERCY

Is every young woman who comes here pregnant?

The girl seated across from my table offers me a tight smile as she rubs her swollen belly. She looks about twenty, with tan skin and big brown cow eyes. She's either visiting a relative or her baby daddy. My gut says it's the latter.

I can only imagine what brought all these people under the roof of Fulcort. What kind of screwed-up lives—shitty parents, roach-infested dwellings, drug-laced nights—would turn tear-filled little boys into hardened, murdering, raping, assaulting villains? And then there are guys like my dad. Good, quiet, hard-working men whose lives crossed paths with those villains in one disastrous night and *they* end up within these walls too. How many of *those* men are trapped in here?

Twenty-two more *years* of driving up to this godforsaken place, sitting in that waiting room for two-plus hours, so I can see my dad for an hour, if I'm lucky. I'll be forty-seven when he gets out. My dad will be seventy-two.

Doing the math hits me with a wave of numbness. How is this my life?

There's a commotion in the far corner. Two guards appear to be directing an inmate and his visitor up out of their seats. They only just sat down at that four-top a few minutes ago, and the inmate is scowling at the smaller table that the guard is pointing them toward. There's a brief exchange of sharp words, and then the inmate, a hulking man with dark skin and a heavy brow, bows his head and marches for the table. His visitor follows.

Moments later, I discover why.

Gabriel saunters through the door, calm as can be. He doesn't pause at the guard with the clipboard for directions on which table he's assigned to. He simply strolls toward that corner, his thumbs hooked in his pockets like he doesn't have a care in the world.

I shake my head as my annoyance flares. I sat out there for over three hours, waiting. This damn guy showed up two minutes ago and he's practically getting valet service. And why? Because everyone is scared of his father. And, maybe, him. Who knows what this guy is into? Drugs, likely. Guns, money laundering? Maybe. I'm no expert in the life of a crime family and what they keep themselves busy doing.

Though, I reluctantly admit that I appreciate the view.

He's dressed much like me, in dark jeans and a black shirt. Except his clothes look designer and expensive and his shirt is fitted and flattering, showing off broad shoulders, cut arms, and that solid, curvy chest.

He likely belongs in an orange jumpsuit, I remind myself. That helps douse the flames beginning to burn in my body, at least for the moment.

Gabriel slows as he passes my table, just long enough to throw a wink my way as if he can read my mind. Heat crawls up the back of my neck as I track him all the way to the corner. The back of him is as appealing as his front—broad shoulders, tapered waist. He has one hell of an ass in those jeans. The kind of ass you get when you live in a gym and lift weights all day long, honing your perfect body.

Wait … he's wearing his watch. The guards made me stuff my necklace, my earrings, my watch—everything metal—into the locker. What the hell! Do *no* rules apply to him and his father?

"Mercy?"

"Huh?" My head snaps back at the sound my father's voice.

I gasp at the sight of him. "Dad!" I cry, the tears springing free.

"Shhh … shhhh … it's okay." He ever-so-slowly eases into his seat with a wince that stretches the ugly gash across his bottom lip.

"It's *not* okay! Who did this to you!" His left eye is swollen and ringed with deep purple and blue bruising. I count five stitches holding the skin over his left cheekbone together.

"Calm down, Mercy," he whispers, and there's sharp edge in his voice. A warning tone.

It's only then that I feel the eyes on us. I rush to wipe the tears from my face as a guard approaches.

"Keep it down, unless you want to lose visitation rights," he warns in a steely tone. Not a shred of sympathy.

I grit my teeth to stop myself from yelling at him. Who *are* these guys they hire to work here? Robots? Can't he understand why I'd be upset? Someone beat the hell out of my father!

"Mercy," my dad warns softly, and I realize that my fists are balled and I'm glaring at the guard with what likely looks like murder in my eyes.

I avert my gaze.

It happens to fall to the far corner, to where Gabriel sits, his hands folded on the table in front of him, watching me quietly, expressionless. He must be able to see my father's injuries from way over there. He must know what's going on. What does he think of all this? Does he think anything at all? Does he care?

"Yo, Skully. How's it hangin'?" a deep, rumbling voice calls out.

The guard who hovers over us nods at the inmate lumbering by—a giant beast of a man with a shaved head and ink covering his scalp—and then, with another warning glare at me, moves back to reclaim his post by the window.

"So? Tell me about your week." My dad forces a smile. He's trying not to wince.

"*My* week ..." A soft, contemptuous chuckle escapes me. Who the hell cares about *my* week?

Not when every week I come here, I have to wonder

what kind of beating my father has survived during *his* week.

"Was it the same guy who did this?"

My dad bows his head and, after a long pause, nods.

Oh my God. When is that going to stop? How much more of this can my father handle?

I find my gaze wandering to the far corner again, unbidden, to where that beastly inmate has settled opposite Gabriel. Gabriel is leaning back in his chair, thighs splayed, smiling easily as he talks, as if sharing a casual conversation with someone over coffee at a Starbucks.

His dark eyes suddenly shift and lock on mine and my heart skips a beat. It's as if he was waiting for my attention.

And, despite my better judgement, I find myself silently pleading with him, begging him to *help* me for my father's sake, because if there is anyone who can help me in this hellhole, it's quickly becoming obvious that it's him.

6 GABRIEL

"When's the next fight?"

"Wednesday night."

"Who against?"

I study Chops's giant paws settled on the table, his knuckles raw from the last beat down he delivered. "Does it matter?"

His deep chuckle rumbles in my chest. "Nah, I guess not."

I've seen Chops—Clarence James, according to his lengthy and impressive rap sheet—in action plenty. Before landing himself in Fulcort for aggravated manslaughter, he used to fight in the underground circuit. He still fights, but on the inside, against the worst of the worst. And the bastard is unstoppable in the ring. He's a dirty fighter, too. I sure as hell would never want him to have a go at me, and I can hold my own.

"And you came all the way up here to tell me? Guard could have sent the message."

I give a casual shrug. "Wanted to check in."

Another deep chuckle, and that ugly mug of his gets even uglier with his grin, showing off his silver grill. I was there the night he lost his four front teeth. The guy who knocked them out is still eating through a tube, a year later. "Bullshit. Whadda you really want, Gabe?"

Chops is a lot of things, but stupid isn't one of them.

"A watchful eye."

His brow furrows. "Who?"

"A new, small fish. He's having a rough entry. I'll pass his deets along."

Speak of the devil … I feel Mercy's big, beautiful eyes on me and I meet them with a steady, knowing gaze. That scene she just caused tells me everything I need to know about her. She loves her murdering father and the sight of him bashed up—damn, Puff's bangers did a number on him—is more than she can handle. And now she's staring at me like a wounded deer caught in a fence, desperate for help but afraid to ask for it from the scary human who approaches.

Clever girl has figured out the pecking order in this place.

Yeah, I know what you want, baby.

But what are you willing to do for me in order to get it?

Because life is all about tit for tat, something she's going to learn soon, if she hasn't already.

"So, you want protection," Chops murmurs. The magic word. And one that costs a shit ton in this world, especially when it's wielded by a guy like him.

"Not yet." I need to make sure it's worth it. "Just a watchful eye for now. Make sure they're not handing out anything he can't walk away from." Translation: make sure they don't kill him.

"What's in it for me?"

Here we go … "Besides all the perks you already get inside here?" I remind him with a severe gaze. His own cell, special meals, extra gym time, extra yard time, fuck time—with females. He's in here for the long haul. Not having us in his corner will make those years seem like hell on earth.

He folds his tree-trunk arms across his chest and meets my gaze, but says nothing.

I sigh. "What do you want?" Tit for tat, and all.

Chops's eyes narrow, as if he's been waiting for the opportunity to ask. "Joyce."

I laugh. "You have to win fights for private time with girls. You know how it works, big fella." The guards bet on Chops, he wins, they win, and they're more than happy to escort a hooker to infirmary and send the nurse on duty away for twenty minutes while the whore rides his dick seven ways from Sunday. "How about some videos that you can jerk off to from the comfort of your cell?"

"Joyce, Wednesday night, after my fight. Win or lose."

Truth is, he could have demanded her anyway, and we'd deliver. And there is no win or lose, because Chops always wins. Maybe he isn't so smart after all.

I grit my teeth, pretending to mull it over for another few seconds. "Fine. But remember, don't step in unless he's going to be peeing through a hose, got it?"

"Yeah, yeah." Chops shrugs. "Who's he to you?"

"Nobody." His daughter, on the other hand …

My gaze drifts her way, to study her pained features as she struggles to carry on a conversation with her father, the shadow of fear casting worry in her beautiful eyes.

That right there is a fucking desperate woman in need of help.

And I'm the only one who can give it to her.

Yes, I think my life is about to get a whole lot more interesting.

7 MERCY

I MAKE it all the way to my battered Corolla outside the prison gates before the dam breaks and the tears begin to stream.

"Can't do anything, my ass," I sob, fumbling for my keys. That's what the guard at the exit doors told me when I asked them how to go about reporting Fleet's cousin—Dad confirmed that's who this guy is—and what they were going to do to stop these attacks from happening. And when I asked to see the security supervisor or warden—anyone—who "could do something," the man chuckled and waved his fingers at me. A "shoo, move along" dismissal.

I unlock my door through blurry eyes and toss my bag in. It's past noon and the desert sun is blistering hot. A wave of heat-stroke-inducing warmth slams into me from my car's interior. It's going to be a *long*, uncomfortable drive home with the windows down today. I peel off my prison visit uniform to reveal the red cotton tank top and Umbra shorts beneath and toss the former into the back seat.

And then I fall into my driver seat, buckling under the weight of my dread.

What state will I find my father in at next week's visit? More gashes? Broken bones? I can't be sure my dad's ribs aren't broken as it is, the way he guarded his right side, the way he was hunched over as he was led back inside. Does this crazy guy not have anything better to do than seek retribution for his vile cousin? Probably not. He's *in prison*. What else is there to do but nurse his anger and exact revenge?

Leaving the door open to release some of the oppressive heat trapped in here, I fold my arms over my steering wheel and lean forward.

And I let myself sob uncontrollably for the first time since this mess all began.

How do I fix this? The appeal process takes years and money. Law school takes years and money and hard work. And neither guarantees anything. The likelihood that I ever get him out of this hellhole early is next to nil.

And he's *all* I have.

"Bad day?" A familiar masculine voice asks from nearby.

My heart begins to race as I swallow a wave of wariness. Gabriel's still here? I vaguely recall him strolling out five minutes after he came in, his "visit" with the giant, scary man brief.

I'm unsure of how I should feel about this guy. I mean, he's a fucking mob boss's *son*. My instincts tell me his hands are far from clean. But he was decent back in the prison when Parker was being a prick, so maybe this isn't a case of "like father, like son"?

Or maybe I'm just too bone-tired and overwhelmed by the state of my life to care anymore.

"You think?" I keep my face buried in my arms as I collect myself, sniffling. "This psycho keeps attacking my father."

"They like to do that in there. Not much else to keep themselves entertained."

"I was just thinking that." I finally peel myself up, wiping my hands across my eyes. In my periphery, I see him leaning against the parked car beside me, arms folded over his chest, legs crossed at the ankle. No doubt I look a sight—my face a red, sweaty mess from crying while sitting in the equivalent of an oven. "He doesn't belong in here. It was an accident. He was just ... I don't know how much longer my father can handle this, and the guards don't seem to care."

"Fulcort has a bad rep for inmate treatment for good reason," Gabriel says.

"That's just great," I mutter bitterly.

"Hate to be the one to break it to you, but this isn't gonna be the last time. It's going to get worse for him."

"No." I shake my head as my eyes burn, refusing to accept that. "There has to be a way to help him. The police or a lawyer or the courts or ... ..." My wobbly voice drifts. None of them helped him up until now.

"They can't help him," Gabriel says, echoing my worst fears. "Inside this place? You need to know the right people and have something they want."

"We don't know anyone. We don't have *anything*." A crappy apartment in a shady neighborhood that half my paycheck goes to, a beater car that will leave me stranded in the hot sun one of these days, and a mountain of debt.

"You sure about that?" There's something in Gabriel's voice—a teasing quality.

I smooth my palms over my cheeks to wipe away the last of my tears and then meet his steady gaze. There's an odd, knowing gleam in it.

Gabriel, the man who can keep the slimy guard Parker in check with a few simple words. Gabriel, who can bypass the wait and stroll to his table of choice. Yes, Gabriel has the power to help me. That much has become glaringly obvious.

But is he standing here now, his fingers absently tapping against his deliciously honed biceps, offering his help to me?

Is he waiting for me to *ask*?

I hesitate, swallowing my nerves. I can't be too proud to ask. Not when it means helping my father. "Do I? Know the right people. Person, I mean," I correct softly.

His steady gaze shifts toward the prison gates, giving me a sublime view of his handsome profile—of that soft mouth, long lashes, sharp cheekbones. "Maybe."

I lick the salty tears from my lips as I consider what my next words should be. *Jesus, what am I doing?* This guy is as good as the fucking mob! Am I *really* about to get myself indebted to him?

This is for my father, I remind myself. And what's a little bit more debt when I'm already drowning in it?

Steeling my spine, I climb out of my car, taking a quick glance around to make sure we're alone, because I doubt these kinds of conversations fall under "legal." My attention stalls on the shiny black Lamborghini purring in the laneway behind my car. He's one of *those* guys. The disgustingly rich ones who drive an ego rocket around town to make sure everyone knows how rich he is.

I push that bitter thought aside. "Would you be able to get this guy to leave my father alone?"

"Yeah." No hesitation.

My heart is pounding with something I haven't felt in so long—hope. I swallow. "I would be forever grateful to you."

That gets an arched brow as his gaze swings back to settle on mine. "Forever grateful?" His lips twist.

"I … don't have any money." I stumble over my words, my cheeks flushing. "We used it all paying for his shitty lawyer. We don't have a house, and I'm driving this thing. But if you'd accept a payment plan or something like that, I'm sure we can arrange something."

Gabriel's gaze drifts to my mouth, where it settles. "How about we start with those lips wrapped around my cock?"

The sting in my palm as my hand strikes his cheek is so sharp that I clench my fist to quell the pain. I gasp, momentarily paralyzed with fear as what I just did sinks in, as I watch the blood spring from the corner of Gabriel's lip.

Aside from Fleet, I've never hit anyone. And now I've gone and slapped Al Capone's son!

But rising to match that fear is rage and disgust. What kind of man propositions a sobbing, desperate woman in a prison parking lot?

A sadistic bastard who saw an opportunity and pounced on it, that's who. And I am now one hundred percent sure that whatever criminal life his father has led, Gabriel is sitting at the table with him, fork and knife at the ready.

"You are a pig," I hiss, my body shaking. "You've clearly mistaken me for a whore, so let me be crystal clear with this: my lips will *never* touch *anything* on you." I can't believe I felt so much as a glimmer of attraction to this creep.

Time seems to stand still as the pink tip of Gabriel's tongue darts out to catch the drop of blood, his fingertip following quickly, as if to confirm that, "yes, that bitch did just hit me hard enough to make me bleed."

Fuck you, yes I did, and you damn well know you deserved it.

My body is stiff as a piece of lumber as I await his reaction.

Will he strike back?

Did I just sign my own death warrant?

There must be security watching over the parking lot. Is anyone watching this now?

A wide, wicked smile surfaces on Gabriel's face, exposing deep dimples on each cheek. Normally, dimples are a weakness for me. On this scoundrel? What a waste.

He nods, as if deciding something. Those midnight blue eyes dip down, over the length of my body, stalling on my skimpy tank top on their way back up. Can he see my heart hammering against its confines?

"Enjoy your week, Mercy," he offers in that deep, seductive voice. He caps it off with a wink and then strolls away to climb into his car, seemingly unfazed.

Not until the engine roars and the car is speeding away do I unlock my knees and let my body sink against the frame of my car.

8 GABRIEL

I ADJUST the lounge chair's headrest for comfort and then will my tense body to relax as I study the vast expanse of stars above.

When Caleb dragged me out to see this house on Camelback Mountain two years ago, I told him he was a fucking moron for wanting to live out of the city. But then the real estate agent walked us through the place—the five-car garage, the two pools, numerous decks, the two-hundred-and-seventy degree view—and I had to admit that I was the moron. We went in halfsies on the fifteen-million-dollar price tag right then and there. I kept my place downtown, but I'm never there anymore, preferring the quiet peace atop this mountain with five acres of space around us and the privacy to do whatever the hell we want.

"Is this good, baby?"

I break my visual game of connect-the-stars to peer down at Lulu, one of Empire's cage dancers. She's perched on the edge of the lounge chair, one fist wrapped around the base of my cock, the other holding her long blond hair to the side to keep it from getting in the way as she sucks me off.

She was already at the house when I got home from Empire tonight, floating topless in the lap pool while Caleb fucked her two friends on the living room couch. Apparently she was waiting for me.

"I'm ready to come," I say.

Her wide lips stretch into a knowing smile, and then she's back at it, her mouth closing over my dick, enveloping it in wet heat as she slides me all the way in until my tip is hitting the back of her throat. And then her head is bobbing up and down, the suction gripping me with renewed fervor.

Blow jobs are Lulu's specialty. The woman was practically salivating when she tracked me down on the balcony off my bedroom. Normally, I'm struggling not to blow my load too soon when she's going to town on me like this.

Tonight though, I'm distracted with thoughts of a raven-haired woman in a tiny red tank top and short shorts. A woman with fire in her tear-soaked eyes, indignation in her steely jaw, and a tremble in her sexy, slender body as she stared me down in challenge.

My tongue darts out to test the split in my lip. Yup, still there.

It's far from the first time I've suggested a woman drop to her knees for me. Sometimes they need a little bit of coaxing—a kiss against their jaw, a suck on their earlobe. Sometimes, like with Lulu, they're already licking their lips as they crawl onto my lap. In the end, I always get what I've asked for.

It's the first time I've ever been slapped for it.

The wave of terror that washed over Mercy was telling, when she realized what she'd done, *who* she'd hit. I expected her to break down in another fit of tears and apologies. Possibly accept my bargain right there in the prison parking lot in broad daylight.

Instead, she seethed, glaring at me in challenge as if to say, "do your worst."

I was already sporting an erection from admiring her long, shapely legs and her perky tits. But that? It made me rock hard. It took *everything* in me to keep from taunting her further to find her breaking point. I haven't been able to get her out of my head ever since.

That does not appeal to me.

I should just forget her and move on, but I already know I'm not going to.

"You not feelin' it tonight, honey?" Lulu presses a consoling kiss on my smooth tip.

Baby, honey … I let the pet names slide because the woman eagerly services me on a regular basis, no questions asked, no strings. Definitely no slaps. But I'm none of those things to her, or anyone else, and I have no interest in being that.

What I *do* have an interest in—more like a rapidly growing obsession—is finding out every detail about Mercy Wheeler's life so I know how best to proceed with this new challenge. Things are only going to get worse for her father and more desperate for her. She needs my help, whether she wants to admit to it yet or not. There will come a point—and soon—where, despite how much she may hate me, she'll reconsider accepting my offer.

I already know she loves her dad that much.

I need to play this differently going forward, though. Mercy is pissed at me, and I can already tell she's not like the other women in my life—she's not going to forget today easily. As much of an arrogant ass as I am, dead fish lying in my bed aren't my thing. I don't fuck women who aren't one thousand percent into it. I want Mercy begging me to fuck her, even as she keeps reminding herself how much she hates me.

I mentally picture what that might look like—that curvy body, naked and splayed on my bed, writhing with need for me.

Reaching down, I grab the back of Lulu's head and yank her down onto my dick, holding her there a moment until she's gagging. Fisting her hair, I roughly guide her up and down as I close my eyes and visualize soulful dark chocolate eyes and the plumpest lips I've ever seen.

Not twenty seconds later, I'm shooting streams of hot cum into Lulu's mouth, biting back the urge to cry out Mercy's name.

9 MERCY

"I DON'T WANT to scare him, but oh my God, he's *so* hot. I'm in love." Michelle's painted crimson lips clamp down on her straw. She sucks back a gulp of Coke.

"*In love?*" I ask, unable to hide the skepticism from my voice.

"Are you kidding me?" she squeals, her fingers flying over her phone's keypad. She shoves the screen in my face to show me the picture of the guy she picked up last night at the club. "Look at him! He's Zac Efron's doppelgänger!"

I swat her hand away. "Yes, yes, you've already shown me, remember?" By way of greeting, as she practically skipped into Mojitos, our favorite Sunday hangout. He's attractive, I'll admit.

"So, how long do you think I should wait before I call him?"

"Long enough for him to have time to cut off that hideous man bun."

Michelle's emerald green eyes sparkle as she bursts

with giddy laughter. "It's horrible, isn't it? But, oh my God, Merce"—her nickname for me rhymes with purse—"he is *such* a good kisser, he can keep the man bun. It doesn't matter to me. He did this thing with his tongue … …" She waggles hers in the air in a way that is far from sexy, making me laugh out loud.

That constant weight on my chest lifts for just a moment, reminding me how long it's been since I've laughed like that.

"*And* he has some seriously hot friends." Her perfect eyebrows arch. "You should have come out with us. You would have had fun. Empire is *so* next-level. No joke."

I met Michelle four years ago in our campus library. She was a bubbly blond eighteen-year-old freshman and she propositioned me on behalf of her then-boyfriend's friend.

Every club that ends in a hookup with a hot guy is next-level for Michelle.

There have been *a lot* of next-level clubs.

"I know." I pick at the taco sitting on my plate. I don't know why I bothered ordering it. My appetite has been nonexistent lately. "I just wasn't really in the mood."

"You're never in the mood anymore." She pouts.

I give her a pointed look.

Her shoulders sag. "I'm sorry. I'm such a brat. How is your dad doing?"

Even thinking about my father makes that lump in my throat swell. "Not good." I tell her about Fleet's vengeful cousin and the most recent beating.

She shakes her head. "It's just so not fair. That guy

tried to *rape* you. I'm glad he got what was coming to him, but your father should not be paying for it."

"I know."

"There's got to be *something* you can do though?"

I snort. "Yeah. I can give Al Capone's son a blow job, and *he'll* help me."

Michelle giggles.

Until she sees my face.

"Oh wait, you were being *serious*?"

By the time I've spelled out all things Gabriel, Michelle's pretty face is pinched with repulsion. "He actually thought that would work?"

"To be honest? It probably does most of the time."

"He's *that* hot?"

"Yeah," I admit reluctantly, though I'm still brimming with enough resentment to dismiss his physical appeal. I was overly emotional at the time, and the blunt, brash proposal shocked me. But the shock has worn off. Now, every time I play the moment back in my mind, I hear those dirty words leave his lip and see the heat in his eyes, and my imagination kicks in and plays the what-if game.

What if I had said okay? What if we had climbed into his fancy car and parked somewhere where he could adjust his seat and unfasten his jeans and pull out what will no doubt be an impressive dick, because how could it not be; he's been blessed everywhere else! What if I took him in my mouth and he stroked my hair and whispered filthy words—he seems the type—until I made him come?

And it's inevitable that every time I play that game,

my heart beats faster, my blood races, my body heats, and a familiar ache stirs between my legs. The fact that I am repulsed by him as a person has not stopped my body from reacting in this way to his physical appeal.

But I will *never* act on it. As far I'm concerned, Gabriel is a troll and I am not paying the fee to cross his bridge.

Michelle's phone chirps with a text. Her gaze flickers to it and then she squeals. "Oh my God! It's him! It's Dean! See? I didn't have to play that stupid waiting game! *He* reached out to me! I've found my prince!"

I chuckle. Michelle is the stereotypical sorority girl—long honey-blond locks, a bright smile, a sexy body—and, while she graduated in spring and is no longer in college, she still lives like she is, hitting clubs any day of the week in stilettos and sparkly dresses that barely cover her ass.

"He wants to meet me at Empire again tonight." She's beaming.

"That's awesome, Michelle. Really." I try to sound like I mean it. It's not that I resent her for how easy her life seems to be. I'm just so tired of how hard mine has become.

Her mouth drops as if she's been struck with an idea. "You're coming with me tonight."

"No—"

"Yes."

"I'll have him bring a friend. You haven't gotten laid in how long? Thirteen … fourteen months?"

My eyes widen. "You've been keeping track?"

"What?" She shrugs. "I'm a good friend! Which is

why I'm making you come out." Her pixie-cute face furrows with worry. "Look, I know things suck for you right now but I miss *my* Mercy, the one with the acerbic wit and the barbed tongue. The tough-as-nails girl who doesn't let life get her down."

"Yeah, well …" I sigh. "Life finally won." That version of me lost steam the day the judge read my father's guilty verdict.

Her voice softens. "I know she's still in there somewhere. We need to find her. You need to find her. Bring her out again. Otherwise, what are you going to do? Just give up on living?"

I pause, her words striking a chord deep inside me.

That's what my mother did. She gave up on living.

"But it's Sunday," I offer as a weak objection. "I have to work tomorrow."

"So do I," she counters.

I roll my eyes. Michelle's father owns a posh jewelry store in Scottsdale. Her "work day" as the "director of publicity" starts whenever she decides to show up— usually around eleven—and consists of posting a few sparkly pictures to Instagram before taking a two-hour lunch break and hitting the gym for the afternoon. She is pint-sized at five foot two but she has a body to kill for.

"Please?" Michelle pleads. "Have one drink and leave by midnight."

"I don't—"

"I *need* you, Mercy." She reaches out to grip my forearm. "What if he's not a prince? What if I'm kissing yet another frog? I need you to meet him and tell me before I *really* fall in love. *Please*. I don't know how many more losers I can take!" She offers a dramatic *Gone with the Wind* hand-to-forehead gesture to emphasize her mock despair.

She *has* dated more than her fair share of dirtbags in the time that I've known her, I'll give her that. And yet she never seems to learn to stop following the hot guy at the bar who's willing to take a drunk girl home.

But a club … "Can't you ask Becky or Tina?" Or any one of her other sorority friends who are no doubt looking to party tonight.

"They don't have good instincts like you. You're my best, most perceptive friend."

I groan. I've always been her black sheep friend—the lower-middle class friend with a mechanic for a father, drowning in student loans.

"Fine. *One* drink, and I'm making like Cinderella at midnight, so," I waggle my finger in front of her, "you have to promise you won't try and guilt me into staying longer."

She makes a cross over her chest. "It'll be fun!"

I sigh. *Fun.* I forget what that is. The truth is, a night out might be fun.

"You'll have to borrow one of my dresses though."

"Uh, no. I have dresses. Ones that aren't completely indecent."

She shakes her head. "Not for this place, you don't. I'm telling you, Merce … Empire is next-level."

———

"THERE BETTER NOT BE ANY STAIRS," I warn Michelle as we ease our way past the bouncers and into the doors of the industrial building-turned-swanky club, the throb of dance music swallowing us up.

"What are you worried about?" She smirks. "You've got granny underpants on."

"Better than floss." Michelle may as well not be wearing *anything*.

"You look amazing, by the way."

"Thanks." I will admit, this backless silver dress I borrowed from her does make me feel like a million bucks, though it's obscenely short. Coupled with these stilettos? I resist the urge to tug at the hem. Yeah, definitely won't pass Fulcort's prison visitation attire rules.

I pause just past a heavy red curtain to take in Empire's interior.

"Told you, huh?" Michelle's glee-filled eyes graze the sea of bobbing heads.

For once, my bubbly blond friend may not be blowing smoke with the next-level thing. This place oozes of money, from the countless ornate chandeliers to the leather banquettes to the giant bird cages suspended from the ceiling, entrapping women in string bikinis and heels grinding to the music.

It's not just the club, though. It's like the patrons are hand-selected from the richest and most attractive. I've never seen so many attractive people packed into one building. There was a line of shiny Porsches and Mercedes waiting for valet service and men in all-black suits flitting about, accepting keys and driving off. And they clearly have strict requirements for who gets to step inside this place. A man in a Honda Civic was trying to valet his car as we approached. The giant bouncer laughed and then dismissed him with a wave of his hand. But the rest of them—well-dressed men and cover-model arm candy—were led right in through the VIP door.

The commoner line to get in? It's wrapped around the block, with two bouncers strolling up and down, dismissing the fools who showed up in jeans and sandals and plucking the most attractive girls for immediate entry.

I balked at that line, ready to turn around and go home. But Michelle grabbed my arm and herded me up to the bouncer at the door.

And wouldn't you know it? He took one look at us and then opened the rope.

After the weekend I've had—and the way my life has been going lately—that gave me a small thrill.

"Dean and his friend Lawrence are meeting us up here!" Michelle slips her hand through mine and leads me toward the bar on the left.

10 GABRIEL

"You've gotta go and see Dad next weekend. He called."

"Fuck that! I just saw him last weekend. *You* visit him this time." I hold the glass of cognac between my finger-tips, waffling with indecision. Do I toss this—and ten more—down my gullet and crash at my condo tonight, or keep it reined in?

I never mess around with getting behind the wheel when I'm drunk. My car isn't exactly inconspicuous. Cops are always looking for a reason to pull a Lamborghini over and the last thing I need to do is give them a valid reason to put me behind bars. My brother and I have been on law enforcement's radar for years. Sure, we have some of them in our pocket, but not *all* of them.

Caleb is a formidable presence standing in front of the one-way office window, arms crossed, studying the crowd at Empire tonight with a deep scowl. "Bad idea, and you know it."

I grunt. He's right. At least I tolerate my father's caustic personality. But Caleb and he are like two bulls running head-on into each other. Two identical bulls—same stubbornness, same explosive temper.

My brother is the one who took the brunt of Dad's anger when we were growing up, when Mom was gone and there was no one there to rein him in. Caleb was bigger than me for a long time. I knew he could take it. Still, I hated watching it happen. He ended up with a few broken bones out of it and a nose that hasn't ever set quite right.

And then one day he hit back.

I thought Dad was going to find his gun and shoot him, but he just grinned wide, slapped him over the shoulder, and said, proudly, "Finally, you're a man."

"Fine. Whatever. I'll go." At least it gives me an excuse to see Mercy again. No doubt she'll be there. I'll have to call ahead and make sure they hold her up until I arrive. Because I'm a jackass like that.

Caleb sighs, rolling his broad shoulders against the growing tension. He's two years older than me and looks a lot like me—we both take after our mother. "The old man's losing it. I wish he'd just accept where he is, step back, and let people run shit how they want to."

I snort. "That won't happen until he's in the ground."

"Here's hoping." My brother lifts his glass and then downs the clear liquid. He'll be drunk by the time we're ready to close, but he always gets one of the girls—whoever the flavor of the night is—to drive his Porsche home for him.

As wrong as it is, I silently toast alongside him. How many problems that would solve.

Something on the main floor catches my brother's eye. "Wow." A low whistle sails from his lips.

"What?"

It's a moment before he responds, his attention transfixed. "I'm looking at my future first wife."

My eyebrows pop. Caleb's favorite hobby is fucking two women at the same time, usually in the ass. The guy hasn't had a girlfriend since he was fifteen, and that lasted a mere week.

I'm no angel, but Caleb uttering the word "wife" should have called forth a lightning strike from above. Commitment is not in the cards for him.

"*This*, I've gotta see." I chuckle, hauling myself up and taking a place next to him. It's another packed house tonight. We only started opening on Sunday six months ago. Before that, it was strictly Thursday to Saturday. We've been at capacity every Sunday ever since. "What are we looking at?"

"Lower bar. This end. Sparkly silver dress. Long black hair."

I search through the sea of bodies until I spot the woman he must be referring to. With that banging body, the back open right down to the curve above her firm ass, it can't be anyone else. "Nice."

"Can you imagine bending that over? Ten grand says she's not wearing panties."

"Ten grand says she'll charge you ten grand to bend over the table."

"Don't call my wife a whore!" He chuckles. "There's no way."

"Maybe you should invite her up so we can find out," I say with mild amusement, because that's something Caleb would do, no maybe about it.

The smoke show reaches up with a slender but toned arm to scoop her silky black hair over her shoulder and then turns to share a laugh with the sexy blond woman beside her, the tiny one hanging off a dude.

My heart begins to pound.

"Fuck *me*."

"Maybe after she fucks me."

"Nah, I mean, I *know* her." I'm *going* to know her. "She's off-limits."

Caleb snorts. "As if."

I level him with a look. "I'm serious, Caleb. She's mine." She just doesn't know it yet.

He twists his lips and regards me a long moment before raising his hands in surrender. "Okay, bro. But you might want to tell her that then, because … …" He nods toward Mercy just as the shmuck standing next to her settles his hand on the small of her bare back and begins grazing his thumb over her skin.

Does she have a boyfriend that I need to get rid of?

Mercy shifts, taking a step away from the guy and his touch.

No. He's just some dumb ass who thinks he has a hope in hell with a girl like that.

"How do you know her, anyway?" Caleb asks, scratching at his jaw, covered in several days' worth of stubble.

I answer him by pointing to the cut on my lip.

"No shit. She's feisty." Admiration sparkles in his eyes. He's always liked the feisty girls.

Feisty … pissed off … I guess I'm about to find out.

I set my full glass down on the desk and march for the door.

"Going to earn yourself another slap?" Caleb asks.

"Probably." But it'll be worth it.

11 MERCY

"Dance with me!" Lawrence yells over the beat, offering me a goofy grin. Dean's friend is attractive—his brown hair shaggy but in a stylish way, his features strong and masculine—but I'm just not feeling anything for him. Also, I'm pretty sure he was drinking somewhere else beforehand because he has been handsy since the second Michelle introduced us. Another strike against him.

I wave his request away. "No, I'm good, thanks. I'm not much of a dancer."

"Aw, come on. I'll teach you." He steps closer, placing a sweaty hand on the small of my bare back for the third time in as many minutes. This time his pinkie slips beneath the low cut of my dress to settle dangerously close to my ass crack.

This guy does not know how to take a hint.

I turn my body as I shift away, dislodging his touch. "Actually, I'm going to head out now. Tired." I reach for Michelle's arm to grab her attention. She's been suctioned to Dean's body since the second he showed up. They've barely said two words to me. The prince or frog verdict is still out. "Call me tomorrow!"

"What?" Michelle takes a break from her fawning to twist Dean's wrist. She frowns at his watch. "But it's not twelve yet!"

"Close enough!" I fake a yawn and then tip my head back to pour the rest of my martini down my throat. There's a gap between the wall of bodies at the bar, and I snake my arm through to set the empty glass down.

"I'll go with her. Make sure she gets home," Lawrence announces, his gaze dipping down the front of my dress.

I shake my head. "No, stay! I'm just going to grab an Uber. It was nice to meet you!" I lie and start shifting away.

"Yeah, so we'll share. We can drop you off at your place first."

Right. So he can follow me into my apartment? "Seriously, I'm *good.*" My annoyance flares.

He slides his fingertips along my bare arm. "Come on … as if I'd let a beautiful woman like you go home alone. Haven't you heard what those drivers do to drunk girls?"

I give him a tight smile. "I'm not drunk."

He shrugs, stepping in closer, forcing me to take a step backward. My back collides with a hard body. I spin around, an apology on my lips.

Where it promptly dies as I find myself face-to-face with Gabriel Easton.

"What are you doing here?" I hiss.

There's no way Gabriel heard my question, but his full lips curl as if he's enjoying my shock. But seriously, what is he doing here? And looking the way he does, his black dress shirt hugging his built frame, unbuttoned at the top to expose his long, thick neck and the hard lines of a sexy collarbone.

Unwelcome heat rolls through my body.

The tip of his tongue darts out to touch the small red cut at the corner of his lip, as if to remind me that I hit him. As if I could have forgotten.

Damn, why does he have to be such a miscreant?

When his eyes shift to Lawrence, they've taken on a decidedly darker, stormier cast than anything I've ever seen. "The lady isn't interested. Back off." Even with the music blasting, I can't miss the deadly edge to his tone as he addresses Lawrence, or the way his square jaw is taut with tension, or how testosterone is practically oozing out of him.

Lawrence, as obtuse as he is, misses the looming threat, puffing out his chest and closing the distance. He's as tall as Gabriel, but as far as physique goes, he's a bone-dry twig at risk of snapping in comparison to Gabriel's hard, muscle-padded body. "Hey, buddy, why don't we let her decide?"

Perfect! Neither of you!

Gabriel's eyebrow arches with amusement as he stares Lawrence down for a few beats before turning to me. He opens his mouth as if he's about to pose the question, but then must think better of it—perhaps on account of the "how about we start with those lips wrapped around my cock" proposition and the hard slap he earned for it.

His gaze drops to settle on my mouth. Yes, that is *exactly* what he's thinking about right now.

My inner thighs clench as the dirty blow-job-in-the-Lambo reel starts playing in my head. Is his dick as perfect as everything else on him? No. It's small. Microscopic. And crooked. Yes. It bends sideways. A ninety-degree angle. It's entirely dysfunctional. No appeal whatsoever.

Gabriel grins, and those sexy dimples appear.

His gaze is still on me as he lifts a hand in the air and waggles two fingers in a come-hither gesture. Two gargantuan bouncers appear out of nowhere to flank him. Gabriel nods at Lawrence.

"What?" Lawrence exclaims, shrinking back as they move in. "What the hell did I do?"

The crowd parts like the red sea for the men as they escort him toward the exit.

"You're kicking him out? He didn't do anything!" Michelle yells. As bubbly as she is, she has no problem calling bullshit where it's due.

Normally I don't either, but my tongue is still caught in my throat.

"He's inebriated and making my female guests uncomfortable," Gabriel says evenly.

My female guests.

"You *own* this place?" I blurt out.

He answers me with an arrogant smirk.

"Oh my God." I groan, my head falling back. Of all the clubs we had to go to … …

Dean is moving toward the exit after his friend, pulling on Michelle's arm to get her to follow.

"Mercy, come on!" she yells, though she's frowning curiously at Gabriel, her eyes dragging over him. I recognize that glint of appreciation.

With pleasure. I take a step toward her, wanting away from this place—and Gabriel—as fast as possible.

He seizes my elbow with strong yet gentle fingers, stalling my escape.

"We have a few things to discuss," he says smoothly, his lips grazing my earlobe, his calloused thumb stroking the back of my arm.

Unease slips down my spine, followed closely by an intoxicating—and unwelcome—rush of blood through my core.

I *really* do not want to be attracted to this creep.

I push aside the thrill of his touch and proximity, and turn to face him. "No, I think we're done here."

His responding laugh makes my palm itch to slap him again. But then the amusement fades, leaving stony features that freeze my limbs. "We haven't even begun."

It sounds like both a threat and a promise, and I don't know if I should be terrified or turned on. Both. I'm both, I accept as my brain scrambles to figure a way out of whatever situation I've gotten myself into.

Michelle suddenly appears beside me. "Do you know this guy?" she yells, her sharp fingernail inches away from poking Gabriel in in the chest.

"No!" I say at the same time that he answers "Yes."

Michelle's eyebrow arches.

He releases me and extends a hand toward her and

offers in a cordial voice, "My name is Gabriel, and I'll be driving Mercy home tonight."

Now it's my turn to look shocked because *hell no*.

Michelle's red-stained lips make a perfect O shape. She lurches forward, pressing her body against mine to shout in my other ear, "*This* is Gabriel? The pervy mob guy?"

"Yeah. He owns the damn club!"

Gabriel's at my other side. There's no way he didn't catch the pervy mob comment, even with loud music. Maybe he'll be insulted by that and finally leave me alone though.

Michelle's eyes dance with excitement. "So, what does he want?"

I spear her with a glare. There's no mystery about what he wants.

She studies him as he patiently waits for us, taking him in from head to toe before pressing her lips to my ear again. "So, all you have to do is blow him and he'll make sure your dad is taken care of?"

"Michelle!"

"What! He's rich and fucking *hot*. Like, I would drop Dean in a heartbeat for a night with *that*."

"Even if the morning finds you in a shallow grave in the desert?"

"Right." Her nose scrunches. "That whole thing."

"Yeah. *That* whole thing."

She loops her arm through mine and then turns to smile sweetly at Gabriel. "Thank you for the kind offer of driving my friend home, but she's coming with me."

The responding smirk—a wicked curl that in no way

implies ease—makes my insides clench. Gabriel closes the distance until there is no space. I'm sandwiched between my best friend and the devil.

Warm fingertips ever so lightly graze the small of my back, making me shudder. "Fine. But I need a moment with her. Alone." There is no mistaking that as a request.

Michelle looks questioningly at me.

The sooner this is over with, the sooner I can go home. So I nod and mouth, "It's okay."

She steps back, releasing her hold on me.

In the next breath, Gabriel's arm hooks around my waist. My body goes rigid as he spins and leads me away, around the side of the bar toward a heavy black door, through the door, past rushing staff, past the noise of a bustling dishwasher station, down a long narrow hall, through another heavy door.

And suddenly we're outside, in a quiet back alley behind the club. The same black Lamborghini from the prison is parked here. Beside it is a cherry-red Porsche.

Oh shit. "Wait, I didn't agree to this." I reach for the door handle and pull. It's locked. My stomach drops. *Shit, shit, shit. I can't believe I fell for this.* Does he really think I'm going to blow him out here? I need to get away from him.

I scan the alley. To my right is a dead end blocked by a chain-link fence. To my left is a street and a security guard. I rush that way, my heels clicking against the pavement.

"I thought you wanted to help your father," Gabriel calls out after me.

"I'm not paying your price." I bite off the "asshole" before it slips out. I'm in an alleyway alone with this guy. No need to antagonize him.

"Maybe my price has changed."

"I told you, I'm not a hooker!"

"I'm not asking you to be."

Despite the wariness slipping down my spine, I slow my retreat. What's he playing at here? Is this just another angle to get me to sleep with him? What else would be in it for him? I don't have anything else to offer besides a twenty-year payment plan.

I sigh heavily. As much as I hate this, I should hear him out. Gabriel has the power to help my father. He seems to be the *only* person who can help him.

Reluctantly, I turn to face him again. "So, what's your new price?" *And why do I feel like I'm going to regret asking?*

His brow furrows. "I haven't decided yet." He pulls a set of keys from his pocket and hits a button. The passenger side door glides opens. "But it starts with you letting me drive you home."

"Do you think I'm stupid? I'm not getting in a car with you!" I scoff.

His dark, smooth chuckle carries through the narrow corridor. "You honestly think I'm going to hurt you? Blondie knows I own the club. If something happens to you, she'll know who to point fingers at when she goes to the cops."

"Unless you disappear her."

His head falls back, and he bursts out with a laugh. "You've watched *way* too much bad crime TV."

My cheeks flush. "Look, I know who your father is."

"Big deal. Everyone knows who my father is." He fixes me with a heavy gaze. "You have *no idea* who I am, though."

A shiver ripples through my body, despite the warm night air. I curl my arms around my body, peeking over my shoulder at my escape route.

"Let me remind you that *you're* the one who physically assaulted me."

"You deserved it."

"I did," he admits, his tongue darting out to graze the cut on his bottom lip, the move utterly sexy.

No, not sexy, Mercy. Nothing about Gabriel is sexy.

"And I'll probably deserve it again before long. But if you want to keep your daddy out of a pine box, get in." That sharp edge in his voice is back, all the more ominous in the oddly quiet alley, the music nothing but a dull, steady thump behind the walls.

Just the mention of my father in a pine box is a punch to my chest.

But going anywhere with Gabriel is idiotic, isn't it?

I waffle indecisively, casting a hand absently toward the door. "My friend is waiting for me."

"Text her and tell her you're getting a ride home with me and that you'll be fine."

Will I, though? If he's not angling for a lay, what else could he possibly want from me? All kinds of warning bells are screaming in my head. *Am I insane for considering this?*

With a heavy sigh, he slips his phone out of his pocket, his thumbs flying over the keypad, the muscles in his forearms cording. "My bouncers are bringing your friend out front now. I'll pull up so you can say goodnight to her. Okay?" Sliding his phone back into his pocket, he strolls over to the passenger side door. And waits, his gaze dropping down to rake over my body, going ever so slowly on my thighs.

His jaw tightens. "Anytime now."

I sigh. Gabriel can help my father.

I'll do anything to help my father.

I guess it's settled then.

I pick my way back, my stomach churning with all kinds of nerves—both the good and bad kind. "Excuse me," I murmur as I approach the passenger side.

He takes the smallest step back, forcing me to brush past him. He offers his hand, palm up. "It's tricky to get into."

"Great," I huff. Especially with stilettos and a dress that barely covers my ass. Ignoring his gentlemanly gesture—we both know he's far from anything resembling a gentleman—I ease into the seat with as much grace as a giraffe trying to lie down. He wasn't kidding; this car is practically sitting on the pavement.

Gabriel's breath hitches and he mumbles something about owing ten grand.

I tuck my legs inside. "What?"

My door shuts before I get an answer, sealing me into his egomaniac-mobile.

Though, I will silently admit, it's impossible not to admire it—all pristine leather and molded surfaces, the gold bull emblem gleaming on the steering wheel. It smells like him, like that spicy cologne that stirred my senses when he sat down next to me in Fulcort's visitor waiting room.

Gabriel slides into the driver side with far more grace than I could muster and fills the seat with a calm arrogance. *So much* arrogance, as if he's the king shit and he runs the world.

With a press of his long, slender finger against a button, the car's engine comes to life. A deep purr vibrates my bones.

"Your address?" he asks, that same finger now poised over the built-in GPS screen.

I hesitate. Do I *really* want this guy to know where I live?

Gabriel sighs with exasperation. "It would take me one phone call to find it."

Something tells me he's not bluffing. And *that* tells me that, if I were as smart as Michelle claims I am, I would be bolting from this car and running down the alley as fast as these stupid stilettos can carry me.

He might actually help Dad, I remind myself.

I recite my address.

"Jesus." He gives me a look of disgust. "Why would you want to live in the slums?"

"Who said I *want* to live there?" I snap, my cheeks flushing with embarrassment. "That's what happens when all your money goes to a shitty lawyer to fight bull-shit murder charges."

Gabriel's eyes narrow. If he's interested in knowing about my father's conviction, he doesn't ask. With the coordinates plugged in, he settles his hand on the shifter and I think we're about to pull out.

Only we don't move.

I dare steal a glance his way, to find his intense gaze locked on my lap, his lips parted. "It's like you've never seen women's thighs before." I tug at the bottom of my dress. I doubt that's the case. How many scantily clad women has he had in this very seat?

"I've seen plenty," he says slowly, and I catch his eyes in the rearview mirror, the dark humor in them. "I've just never wanted to bury my face between them so bad before."

I can't stifle my gasp at that bold admission. My legs clench together, his lewd suggestion stirring unwanted need in my core. "You were right about deserving another slap before the night is through." My voice sounds strangled.

He throws the car into Drive. "And I gave you that one. Don't do it again."

"Or what, you'll hit me?" What is wrong with me tonight? It's as if I'm *trying* to provoke him into anger.

My body jolts with the sudden halt of the car.

"Let's get one thing straight right now, Mercy." Gabriel's voice has turned icy. "Whatever you think I've done, whoever you think I am … I am *not* going to hurt you. I am not going to lay a finger on you, unless you ask me to." His eyes blaze as they regard me through the darkness. "You got that?"

I manage a feeble nod, because everything about him right now suggests otherwise.

We crawl along the alleyway and turn right when we reach the street, Gabriel carefully steering his car around a pothole that would no doubt damage the undercarriage. We coast past the long line to get in, and his car has the desired effect. People gawk as Gabriel bypasses the valet line and pulls up in front of the main entrance, where Michelle, Dean, and Lawrence wait.

When my window slides down at Gabriel's control and Michelle sees me in the passenger seat, her mouth drops open. Dean looks equally impressed. Lawrence, who is standing next to him and scowling at the sports car, does not.

"So … there you are!" Michelle manages. "I was worried."

"Sorry. Gabriel's giving me a ride home." His name is becoming familiar on my tongue, the same way the name of a guy you've just started seeing becomes familiar. I don't like this one bit.

"I see that." She bobs her head, stunned. But then she snaps out of it, demanding, "Text me as soon as you get home! And remember … …" Her green eyes widen knowingly.

"Yup." *Use the code*. The texting code we came up with one night while drunk and playing the "what if one of us goes home with a hot guy who turns out to be a psychotic murderer and he makes us text our friends to lie and say we're okay but really we're being held captive" game. We agreed to use codes—"best night of my life" really means "call 911 and trace my phone because I'm about to be chopped up into bits," and "it's all good" to say we're about to get laid.

We never did pick a phrase for the third option—the "I don't think I'm going to be murdered but I am definitely not putting out for this asshole" code.

With that, my window rolls up and we take off again, the engine roaring to life as Gabriel deftly navigates the luxury car away from Empire.

I keep my phone gripped tightly in my hand as I curl my arms around my chest to ward off the chill inside the car. Should Gabriel decide he's not taking me home but somewhere else, I will be texting a mayday to Michelle.

Gabriel dims the air conditioning with a stroke of his finger. "Better?"

"Yeah," I mutter.

"You sure? You're covered in goose bumps."

"They'll go away." Is he *always* so attuned to his passenger's body? Or is it because his gaze keeps drifting from the road to my legs? God only knows what other dirty thoughts are going on in that beautiful head of his.

The GPS directs us onto the freeway that leads to my neighborhood. So far, so good.

I note all the rubberneckers as we pass the other vehicles, their envious eyes taking in the shiny sports car. "So you're an attention whore."

He smirks. "Why would you say that?"

"Why else would you drive a car like this?"

"Because I can. Because I like fast, powerful things. Because I can do *this*." Suddenly he's cutting across three lanes and gunning the engine. In seconds we're flying past everyone else, mere flashes of light on the road.

"Okay, you've proven your point," I say through gritted teeth, my body tensing. "Please slow down."

"Why? Is this scaring you?"

"Of course it's fucking scaring me! I'm not a fool

with a death wish!" I snap, bracing myself with one hand on the door, as if that'll make a lick of difference if someone decides to cut into our lane ahead. And yet I got in the car with a fool with a death wish.

With a chuckle, he eases off the gas pedal and changes lanes.

I let out the lungful of air I was holding. "Look! That might impress the insipid females you normally have in here, but it doesn't work on me."

"Good. I'm glad," he says, and I note something odd in his voice. Genuine happiness, I think. As if he's pleased that I shrieked at him. "Who do you live with?"

"No one. I lived with my father, but now … no one."

"Your mother?"

"She passed away when I was ten."

He pauses. "How?"

"She was sick." My mother's cause of death is not one I broadcast freely.

"Hmm." In my periphery, I catch his slow nod, as if he's cataloguing it in the Mercy file, but nothing else follows. No "I'm sorry," no "that's terrible." "Do you have a job?"

"What's with the small talk? I already know what your angle is."

"Just making conversation. I'm curious about you."

"Fine. Let's make conversation then." I ignore that voice in the back of my head, the rational one that warns it's not a good idea to question a guy from a crime family about all the illegal shit he's into. "Are you a criminal like your father?"

His eyebrows pop. "You call that small talk?"

"What's wrong? Afraid to answer?" I taunt. I've officially gone mad.

He switches lanes and eases off the freeway. "I'm a businessman. You remember that club you just left? That's mine. Well, half. My brother and I are partners."

"*Really*. That's *interesting*. And how could you afford a place like that? You're what, twenty-six? Twenty-seven?"

He chuckles. "Twenty-nine, actually. But thanks for the compliment."

"I wasn't trying to compliment you. I was proving a point. What funded your little club? Guns? Drugs? Prostitution? All of the above?"

"My family comes from money," he responds smoothly.

"*Right*." I snort. "I've read the news. Your father is in jail for laundering money. Why would you need to launder money if you weren't doing anything illegal?"

His smile catches me off guard. "You seem awfully interested in my father. I guess I've misread these looks you keep giving me. Do you want me to introduce you to him? Maybe I can arrange some private time at Fulcort, in one of the rooms—"

"No, thanks." I feel my face pale at that idea, quickly followed by a wave of nausea.

Gabriel says nothing more, making a right turn at the intersection.

"You know, a sane person wouldn't head into this part of Phoenix with a car like this at night. We're liable to get jumped by gangbangers."

"I'm not worried," he says, and by the calm in his voice and the relaxed way he sits, I can tell he's truly not. "So you're studying for the LSAT. How are you paying your bills now that your father is gone?"

"He's not gone!" The choice of words ignites my panic. Gabriel makes it sound like my father is dead. He's not. "He's just ..." *Gone.*

For the next twenty-two years, he will not be in my life aside from the hour I get with him every Saturday at Fulcort. The reality of that is beginning to sink in, and it makes me want to puke.

"How are you paying your bills, now that your father is in prison for the foreseeable future," Gabriel amends.

Suddenly I don't have the energy to avoid the inquisition. What's more, I just don't care to. "I work full-time as an office assistant at Mary's Way, and I'm almost finished my degree. I was going to become an addiction counselor, but shit happened and now I'm going to try to get into law school so I can become a lawyer and get my dad out of prison."

"An addiction counselor. *Why?*" His tone says "why would you want to be one of those?"

"Gee, I don't know ... to *help* people?"

He still looks baffled.

I roll my eyes. I shouldn't be surprised that that concept eludes him. "Anyway, plans have changed."

"Because now you want to help your dad."

"I *need* to help him." My gaze drops to my nail—the polish chipped only hours after Michelle painted it for me—as I swallow away my dread.

Gabriel sucks in his bottom lip. "And why do you think you can actually get him out of prison?"

"Because he didn't *murder* anyone! He was defending

me. I have to do something, or he'll be stuck in there for the next twenty-two years! If Fleet's cousin doesn't kill him first."

"Fleet?"

"The guy my dad killed." *The guy who attacked me.*

Gabriel's handsome face twists. "Stupid fucking name."

A weak chuckle escapes me. "I can't believe it. We agree on something." I remember thinking the same thing when I walked up to Billy's Wreckers that day to bring my dad lunch and met the then-new guy. That's the day his sick obsession with me began.

I ignore Gabriel's scowl of disgust as he eases his car over the curb and into the driveway of my apartment complex. Up ahead, a police car is parked behind my Corolla, its red-and-blue lights flashing. Two beefy blond officers are standing beside it, having a heart-to-heart with Bob, who's in nothing but his briefs, holding an ice pack against his forehead.

"Not again … …" Rita always goes on the warpath after the police show up, banging on doors, demanding to know who called the cops on them. Between her and Glen's late-night Doritos visit, I'm not going to get any sleep tonight.

"I take it having the cops visit is common around here?"

"At least twice a week. Three times if Micky Hansen on the second floor is in the flashing mood." The old man's ball sac hangs halfway down to his knees.

Gabriel's jaw tenses as the two cops turn around and

eye his car suspiciously. As they should. A car like this has no business here.

For the first time, Gabriel looks on edge.

"What's wrong? Worried they'll search your car and find something they shouldn't?" I ask sweetly. Is he dumb enough to be driving around with kilos of drugs? How does that whole operation work anyway? Does he ever see the drugs or does he have people to do it?

So many questions.

He slides into a visitor parking spot and shifts into Park, leaving the engine purring. "The police don't worry me at all. I've done nothing wrong." He turns in his seat to offer me an infuriating smile. "But you're going to have a hard time convincing them that you aren't a high-class hooker."

The way I'm dressed … where I live … climbing out of this car … …

Shit. Gabriel's not wrong.

And the way those cops are looking this way, they're probably thinking the same thing. "Well, maybe I'll tell them you just finished paying me to suck you off." I make a point of dragging the tip of my tongue over my bottom lip, then my top.

Gabriel's eyes burn as they follow the action. "If you're going to do that, you might as well commit the crime."

"You going to whip your dick out right here? With the cops standing twenty feet away?"

His hand falls into his lap to cup himself. It's too dark to see if he has an erection, but by the way his breaths are growing more shallow and quick, I'd say so. "You dare me to?"

"Sure."

He reaches for his belt and pauses, his gaze dropping to my mouth.

I realize I'm biting my bottom lip in heady anticipation.

Shit.

His hand falls away. "You'd probably chew on me."

"Not probably," I throw back, trying to shake this sudden, depraved sexual tension floating between us.

He peers out his window at my humble abode.

I can't take it anymore. "So, about my father ... have you decided whether you're willing to help me?"

"I've always been willing to help you." His dark gaze shifts to me, sliding down my neck, over my chest, onto my lap. "But you have to pay the price."

"And what is that price?" I ask through gritted teeth. The bastard keeps toying with me. He smiles. A wicked smile, and I know I'm not going to like what I'm about to hear.

"Stay with me."

12 GABRIEL

I HAVE NEVER WANTED to go to town on a woman's pussy as much as I do right now. That dress is an inch from being indecent—my favorite length. It would take nothing to reach over the console, slide aside those white lace panties that I caught a glimpse of as Mercy was trying to get into my car, and push two fingers deep inside her.

I've done it a hundred times in this car. The difference is those women were always willing, their thighs parting in invitation the second their asses hit the leather. But Mercy has kept those slender, toned thighs locked tighter than a bank vault the entire drive home.

It's made my dick rock-hard.

And now we're sitting outside her dump of an apartment, with two patrol cops seconds from coming over, and she's staring at me like I just told her I'm an Amish woman.

"*Stay with you?*" She repeats the condition I just decided on minutes ago, the second I saw where she lives. Her mouth twists over the words as if they taste off. "What does that mean?"

"Exactly what it sounds like. I have a place on Camelback." *A palace compared to this shithole.*

"But ... but ... *why?*"

Because by the time I'm done with you, you'll be begging me to fuck you.

The thought has my dick straining against my zipper.

Oh, she hates me all right. She's already made up her mind about who I am—she isn't necessarily wrong—and I am the dirt beneath her shiny, sexy shoes. No, I'm worse than dirt. I'm a pile of dog shit she accidentally stepped in and can't seem to scrape off.

My car, my club, my body ... *none* of it impresses her.

And yet she's attracted to me. The way she clenched her thighs when I told her I wanted to bury my face between her legs? I know women's bodies. That wasn't a "I'd rather set my pussy on fire than have you touch me" squeeze—not that I've ever had a woman react that way to me. But there was no mistaking the shift and slow rub to quench a sudden ache.

She's attracted to me; she just doesn't want to be. Which means we're going to have hate sex. I'm okay with that. In fact, I'm *more* than okay with.

"Why?" she pushes.

Because your life is falling apart.

Because you need help and I can help you.

Because I haven't been able to get you out of my fucking head since I first saw you.

"Because it's my deal. Take it or leave it."

Her chocolate-brown eyes search my face, then her car, then the dim rust-orange doors of the apartments in her roach-infested building, as if considering it. "For how long?"

"A week," I blurt out, because it's the first thing that comes to my mind, adding, "or until I say you can go. But not more than a week." I'm sure she'll be out of my system before then.

She frowns as she tries to wrap her head around my twisted demand. And it is twisted, I'll be the first to admit that. I just don't give a shit.

"So, like … I'm going to be a *prisoner* in your house?"

I chuckle. "You can still go to your classes and your job." *A thankless, low-paying job catering to junkies who will eight out of ten times fail all your hard work.* Who is this chick trying to be? Mother Theresa? "But outside of that, when I'm home, you're home." Ideally naked, but we'll work our way up to that.

Her eyes narrow. "Where would I sleep?"

"Like I said …" I match her steely gaze. "You'd be staying *with me*." In my king-sized bed.

Ideally, naked.

Rage flares in her big eyes. "But you're *not* asking me to be a whore, right?"

"No. I'm not. You don't have to fuck me." I can't keep the grin off my face as I add, "But, trust me, you'll want to."

"*Never.* Fuck you," she spits out. Grabbing her purse, she hits the door release and the door slides open. She's out of my car with surprising ease, fishing for her key as she rushes for the stairs to her apartment, those sexy calves straining with the height of her shoes.

"Miss? How are you this evening?" one of the officers calls out in that cordial way that means he's fishing for someone to bust. "Is something the matter?"

"I'm fine!" she snaps. "And he's a pig." She throws a hand my way. "I wouldn't blow him if he offered me a *million* dollars!"

I groan softly.

She has one hell of a temper, that one. It's not helping the cock strain. Maybe it's a good thing the police are here, because I'd probably do something dumb like climb out of my car and chase after her. There's no need for that. She loves her father and it's becoming clear that she'll do anything for him.

And when those guys *really* start working him over—because my guess is they're just warming up—she'll come crawling to me.

Right into my sheets.

I'm smiling even as one of the cops begins strolling my way

13 MERCY

I sɪɢʜ with relief as I spot a prison guard with a bushy mustache sitting behind the visitor's registration desk when I rush in. I don't have the stomach to deal with Pervy Parker right now. My day has already been shit. I should have arrived at Fulcort hours ago but my car overheated on the freeway halfway here and it took forever for Billy from my dad's garage to come and tow me back. Thank God he lent me his pickup so I could still visit my dad.

I step into line—it's busy today—and check my phone for the time. Eleven fifteen. Plus another two to three hours of waiting, if history is any indication.

I hope Dad doesn't think I bailed on him.

I stifle my sighs of impatience and roll on the balls of my feet as I wait for the four people in front of me take their turns signing in. Mustache Man isn't in any rush. By the time I find myself in front of him, I'm on edge.

"Mercy Wheeler, here to see Duncan Wheeler." I

pass over my driver's license for ID. I'm becoming a pro at this whole prison visitor thing.

"Duncan Wheeler … …" My father's name drags from his Midwestern accent as he scribbles it down on the log before setting his pen down and shifting to the computer to verify my credentials and that I'm an approved visitor.

I study the bushy gray thing above his lip as he punches in keys with his two index fingers. The tips of the whiskers closest to his mouth are stained pasta sauce-red. Will that just wash out? Or does he have to trim every time he eats spaghetti? How much food does he get caught in there on a regular basis?

"Sorry. No visitors for that inmate this week," he announces in a monotone voice.

I frown. "What do you mean? Why not?"

"I mean you can't see him today. He's recovering in the infirmary."

My stomach drops. "Recovering? Excuse me, what does that mean? Is he *hurt*?"

"That would be my guess." He sets my ID on the counter in front of me.

"But … how? When? Is it bad?" I sputter, my voice turning shrill. "Why didn't I get a call?"

He sighs with forced patience. "Miss, we don't usually call next of kin unless there's a body to claim."

Pervy Parker lumbers over then, a half-eaten banana in his grip. "Merc-*y*, guess you just heard? They brought him back last night."

"Back from *where*?" I hear the desperation in my voice as cold dread washes over me.

"Dude's been in the hospital since last Sunday." He says it so casually.

"Last Sunday!" The day after I saw him? He's been at the hospital *all week* and *no one told me?*

Parker settles into the seat that Mustache Man just vacated. When he looks up at my face, he must finally clue in that I may not be taking this news well. "Oh, don't worry, sweetheart. He's doing fine. Breathing on his own again and everything."

Breathing on his own and …

The room starts to whirl.

My legs buckle.

I'm vaguely aware of strong arms grabbing hold of me as I go down, and then I'm aware of nothing at all.

——————

I BLINK REPEATEDLY against the haze of oblivion.

Chalk-white walls.

Cold flickering lights.

"Where am I?" I mumble out loud to no one in particular, struggling to focus.

"Fulcort. In the room where they perform strip searches," a familiar male voice purrs, the hilarity in his voice thick.

It takes a split second before I clue in that the pillow beneath my head is in fact not a pillow, but Gabriel's lap.

I bolt upright. My head spins with the sudden movement.

"Relax, or you'll pass out again," he warns calmly.

I'm stretched across a row of four hard blue plastic chairs. They're not in the least bit comfortable. The room we're in is tiny, plain, and white, empty of everything but these chairs and a trash can in the corner.

My memory snaps into place like a rubber band. "My father was attacked again."

"Nothing he won't recover from." Gabriel is studying a hangnail.

Did Parker say that? The last thing I remember was him saying that he's breathing on his own again.

Squeezing my eyes shut, I give my head a few seconds to stop its swimming before reopening them. My mind is still swirling though. "Why are you here?" It's been six days since Gabriel dropped me and that absurd proposition off at my doorstep.

His dark chuckle skitters along my spine. "You're not the only one with people to visit, remember?"

Right.

"It's a good thing I came, though," he says after a moment. "Otherwise Parker would have been the one to collect you off the floor. He'd be in here with you."

I shudder at the thought. God knows what that sicko would have done to my unconscious body.

Then again, I'm in here with *this* sicko. A quick glance down at my T-shirt and jeans confirms that my clothes haven't been disturbed.

"Unconscious women don't get me off," Gabriel says, as if he can read my thoughts.

Swinging my legs off the chairs, I take a few moments to ground myself, sliding my running shoes across the tan industrial tile. There's a fine film of sand on them, and my soles make a scratching sound. "And they just let you wait in here with me? Why?"

Gabriel stretches his long legs out beside mine. "Haven't you figured that out yet?"

Because he told them to.

Because Gabriel gets whatever he wants.

And he wants me.

What must it be like, to have such power and influence? Not enough to avoid prison for his father, but certainly enough to get whatever they want while he's in here.

I steal a glance Gabriel's way. He's like an advertisement for "sexy chill"—slouched in his chair, his deliciously honed arms folded across his broad, hard chest, his aviator sunglasses tucked into the collar of a pristinely white T-shirt, his tapered waist leading into a pair of dark wash jeans that hug his hips in an appealing—

There is prominent bulge beneath his zipper.

Oh hell. Did he spring an *erection* while I was lying here unconscious? If not, that is one impressive dick.

That familiar and unwelcome jolt stirs in my body as I peel my gaze away from his lap to his face, where I find his lips curled in a dark, sexy smile, the kind that tells me he knows exactly what I was admiring.

My cheeks burn.

This guy is the son of an infamous crime boss. He's filthy rich and morally corrupt. Scratch that; corrupt in *every* way possible. He's disgusting.

He's also devastatingly handsome. I'm sure there are plenty of women—stunning women—who are more than happy to disregard his illicit daily activities, too busy ogling him and his fancy car. But *I* am not one of them. I've made that clear.

So why does he keep showing up in my life like this?

"What do you want with me?" I hear myself whisper, though I'm pretty sure I already know. He's demanding that I stay in his house—that I sleep in his bed. Only a fool wouldn't equate that to sex, despite that bullshit about not treating me like a whore.

His responding smile says as much. It slips off though, replaced by a curious frown. "Why were you just checking in now? You're usually here early."

"My car broke down on the freeway. I had to wait for a tow and borrow a car ... ..." My answer fades as his question sinks in. "How do you know I'm usually here early?"

"Because the guards told me. I had them keep you in the waiting room until I showed up last weekend." He admits this as if it's normal. As if he was doing me a favor and I should thank him.

My frustration explodes. "Do you think this is a game, Gabriel? It isn't! It's my life!"

"Actually it's your father's life," he smoothly answers, as if the emotion in my voice doesn't affect him at all.

My father. God, my poor father.

"They won't let me see him." I pinch the bridge of my nose against the blossoming headache. "They won't even tell me what happened."

He sighs. "Guys jumped him, during dinner." There's at least at touch of sympathy in his voice now.

"When his ribs shattered, one of the bones punctured his lung."

"Oh my God." Tears burn my eyes, images of my father curled in a fetal position while "they" kicked and punched him repeatedly. "Fleet's cousin again?"

"Sounds like it. They put someone in the hole."

I sigh, my shoulders sagging with relief. "At least they're doing *something*." At least *some* of the guards care about the safety of the inmates. "Thanks. For finding that out."

And for not leveraging that information. He could have baited me into blowing him in this private room before he shared it. And honestly? As overwhelmed and tired and beaten down as I'm feeling right now? He might have won that round.

"You're welcome, Mercy." The sentiment is delivered on a honeyed tongue, my name somehow sounding dirty.

I fall back in my seat, resting my head against the wall. "At least my dad will get a break."

"For another week or two, while he's laid up in sick bay. They'll put him back out the second he's walking. From there … well, hopefully this Fleet guy and his buddies lay off until he's a hundred percent, otherwise I'd hate to see where your dad ends up the next time."

I squeeze my eyes shut. The next time. There *will* be a next time. And Gabriel is making sure I don't doubt it. This is all part of his twisted plan to get what he wants from me.

"You ready to ask for my help yet?" His voice is soft as he goes in for the kill.

I stare at my shoes as a hot tear rolls down my cheek, followed by a second … and a third … and I accept that I'm out of options. I need to grab hold of this lifeline, no matter the cost.

It's just a week. Unless he gets bored of me before that. I'm counting on that.

"Will you protect my father?" I whisper, unable to meet his gaze, the weakness in my voice seeming like a scream. I hate it, but I don't have the energy to guard against making myself so vulnerable. I *am* vulnerable.

Gabriel knows it and, the sadistic bastard that he is, he's willing to take full advantage of it.

But whatever … If it keeps my father safe, I'll close my eyes and welcome him with spread legs every night. I guess it could be worse. He could be a Fleet or a Parker, or some other repulsive reptile. At least this snake is disguised as an Adonis.

I feel his gaze on me. "Glad you're finally seeing reason."

There is nothing *reasonable* about any of this.

I tense with anticipation as Gabriel leans toward me, until I realize that he's merely shifting in his seat to reach into his back pocket. He produces a business card and holds it out for me between his two fingers.

It's a moment before I reach for it, pinching the far end, careful not to make contact with him.

"Address is on the back. Be there by eight tonight, *sharp*. Security will be expecting you. Bring your things." His voice is suddenly cool, all business.

I'm doing this. I'm actually doing this.

"Wait." I meet his gaze. "What exactly does protection mean? What are you going to do?"

He stares hard at me for a long moment. "Do you need details, Mercy? Do you *really* care?"

About this cousin gangbanger of Fleet's who's going to kill my father?

Right now, I want the bastard dead.

I swallow. "No, I guess not."

With that, he eases out of his seat.

"Why are you doing this? I'm not your type, remember?"

"Maybe I like a good challenge."

You twisted mother … My anger flares. "I may be agreeing to this, but don't expect me to be pleasant. I can't fake it."

"Good, because I've never had a woman fake *anything* for me."

I let out an unattractive snort. "That you know of."

"Trust me, I *do* know." His deep chuckle grates on my nerves. "And you'll find out soon enough."

And we've slipped into talk of sex. When I'm *begging* him for it? Never. Not in a million years. I let the bitter smile stretch my lips. "You're going to be highly disappointed."

His gaze lingers on my mouth. "I don't think either of us will be disappointed." With that, he strolls out the door.

And I stare at the card in my hand—at the tidy penmanship on the back of an Empire business card, directing me to an address on Camelback Mountain. He had it at the ready, like he knew what was going to happen today, like he knew I'd break.

But isn't that the way with men like this, who *always* get what they want?

And now I'm going to be staying with him in his house—in his bed—for the next seven nights.

14 GABRIEL

"You come when I tell you to, not when you feel like it, you little shit," my dad snaps by way of greeting. He jams his hefty body into the molded seat of the visitation table.

"Sorry," I offer, though my voice doesn't relay that. Because I'm not. "Got caught up with a problem."

"What kind of problem?"

"A personal one." Today couldn't have played out more perfectly had I orchestrated it myself. I made it to Fulcort earlier than usual, with a slight spring in my step knowing that Mercy would be here and that Parker would hold her until I arrived.

The dumb prick didn't mention anything about her father being hospitalized and unavailable for a visit.

Had Mercy not had car troubles, she would have received that news this morning. She would have left by the time I came in. I definitely wouldn't have been there in time to catch her as she started to slump.

I wouldn't have had the chance to cradle that sexy,

tight body in my arms and carry her into that private room and ever-so-softly trace the shape of her jaw with the pad of my thumb as I waited for her to come to.

She wouldn't be on her way home to pack her things as we speak.

Yes … today could not have gone any better for me.

Other than the fact that I have to sit here and deal with my father sneering at me.

"You wanted me here. I'm here. What's the problem?" I ask before he has the chance to lay into me.

"I want you and Caleb to have a conversation with Camillo Perri. We have a common interest. It's time we joined efforts to deal with our *friends*."

"Perri?" I feel my face twist up as I spit that name out. "*That* two-headed snake! Are you out of your damn mind?" The Perri and Easton families have feuded over money and power for decades, our territories overlapping each other, and neither of us willing to concede on who was playing the drug game first. There's enough bad blood between us to last five generations.

Camillo Perri is the reason my mother is dead.

If there is one thing I know, it's that he would throw his own children to a pack of hungry wolves to give himself a head start. Getting in bed with him in order to deal with the cartel will only guarantee my brother and me a cell in Fulcort, and we have way too many years of life left to enjoy to risk rotting in here.

"No." I accentuate it with a firm head shake.

"No?" My father's eyebrows arch. "Did you just say no to *me*?"

"It's a bad idea," I amend, adjusting my tone, but

only slightly. "And Caleb will never go for it either. Not after Mom."

My father's brow tightens, the only sign that her death still affects him. "Retributions were paid."

I grit my teeth. "Not to Caleb and me, they weren't." Because no amount of money or eye-for-an-eye bloodshed will ever be enough for us. "Have you talked to Uncle Peter about this?"

Dad waves a meaty hand. "Fuck your uncle Peter." His scowl tells me all I need to know.

Our uncle hasn't been returning my father's calls since they last met.

"Perri will be interested in entertaining a truce," he asserts. "It's in his best interest to."

Yeah, and then it'll be in his best interest to stab us all in the back.

"We need to stop these vultures before it's too late. They're coming in to peck away at all that I've built because they know I'm in here and they think we're weak. I need you two out there, reminding them of how we do business."

"Too much risk with Perri."

"*Everything* we do has risk," my father snaps.

Not the club, I want to say, though that's not entirely true. Plus, Dad doesn't give a shit. All he sees is his own empire crumbling, and he has too much pride to let that happen. "Go see him. And have good news for me next time you come in." Dad slaps the table as if hammering his gavel. He hauls his body up and lumbers away, leaving me to roll the tension from my neck.

Fuck this shit, Caleb's coming the next time. They can kill each other with their bare hands for all I care.

I want to get as far away as possible from this place as I can, but there's one more person I need to talk to.

I nod at Sunni, a brawny, balding guard who lives with his mother and has made serious cash bets on the prison fight club circuit. He responds with a chin lift and then a hand gesture to another guard.

Five minutes later, Chops is settling into the seat my father vacated.

I take in his swollen left eye, the bruising around it an angry deep purple. "Heard you put on a shitty show last Wednesday."

He grins. "I let him have one before I put him down." He cracked his opponent's skull in under a minute, is what he did.

"You keep pulling that kind of shit and nobody's gonna be willing to fight you. You know what that means." No more fights means no more winnings for the guards or for us, which means no more perks for Chops.

His responding chuckle is downright sinister. "Place like this? Someone's always willin' to fight and you know it."

Yeah, I know it. That doesn't mean the paying viewers don't want a show. But this isn't why I called him here. "Speaking of fighting ..." I cock my brow.

"Your new fish?"

"I told you to keep him on his feet. I was clear, wasn't I?"

His lips twist. "Guy's not built for a little tussle, I guess."

I level him with a hard look. "That's why you were supposed to be there." To make sure my leverage over Mercy didn't get carried out in a body bag.

Chops holds his massive hands in the air, palms up. "Hey. You either want protection or you don't. This in-between 'just watch' shit? It don't work well. You feel me?"

"Yeah. I feel you."

Deceptive bright blue eyes size me up. "So, what's it gonna be?"

I need Duncan Wheeler to survive beyond the next week or two.

"To start, you're gonna send a message."

15 MERCY

THE SECURITY GUARD scowled at my Corolla as I pulled up to the Cactus Hills entrance gate at ten to eight and handed him my ID. He asked if I was a housekeeper, to which I curtly replied no.

His scowl deepened, as if any other scenario did not compute, but he didn't push, jotting down my license plate number and waving me through.

Now, as the voice on my phone's GPS spits out directions and my car chugs along the winding street up the mountain, I think I can understand.

Gabriel lives in a luxury estate community. And by luxury, I mean rich-ass folk with more money than they know what to do with. Mansions built into Camelback Mountain's humps, each surrounded by acres of privacy. No one but scullery staff would frequent these houses in a car like this.

Or maybe not even, I note, passing a woman in a shiny red Audi with a maid service magnet affixed to her car.

"You have arrived at your destination!" chirps my GPS.

I pause on the street to take in the modern design of sharp angles and excessive windows. The massive house is at least three levels. Maybe more, given it's built into the mountain. I don't know what I was expecting, but it's stunning, I admit begrudgingly.

Flutters stir in my stomach as I turn into the long paved driveway. Five steel garage doors sit in a tidy row ahead of me.

Five.

Because I guess an arrogant man with a Lambo needs that many. The shiny sports car—or any car for that manner—is nowhere to be seen. I'm surprised. I took Gabriel for the kind of guy to park it in prime view for casual passersby. Shine spotlights down on it to make sure it isn't missed. That sort of thing.

My car comes to a sputtering halt in front of the farthest door. I turn the key and the engine cuts off abruptly, and I'm not entirely sure that it didn't just die. Wouldn't that be perfect. When I drove Billy's truck back to the shop after visiting Fulcort, Billy was reluctant to hand me my keys, saying that the Corolla needed *a lot* more work before it would be considered road safe, and that I should *really* consider investing my money into a more reliable beater.

What money?

I smiled and thanked him for sourcing the needed parts so quickly—and for not charging me for labor— and then I raced home to try and grapple with the gravity of what I'm about to do.

"This is no big deal," I whisper out loud, giving myself a pep talk. "Think of it as a drunken one-night stand. You've had those before." Three, to be exact. Sexy, thrilling, exciting encounters with hot men that quickly led to sloppy, sweaty fuck fests that ended in head-pounding, cotton-mouth mornings of shame, my dirty panties tucked in my clutch as I angled for the fastest escape plan.

I regretted every single one of them.

And I picked those guys up at a club. I *chose* them. Gabriel belongs in the prison where he found me, and I haven't chosen any of this. Maybe that's what gets him off most about this situation though—that he has all the control and I have none. He may not be forcing me into anything, but he damn well knows I'll do anything to help my father.

I need to find a way to take control.

I should just walk in there, drop my clothes, and fuck him. He wouldn't be expecting that. And with guys like him, the sooner he sleeps with me, the sooner he'll get bored of me, and the sooner I can go back to my shitty life, father saved.

I note the security camera at the corner of the garage, pointed downward over the driveway. Is Gabriel watching me right now? Is he sitting in his house with that sexy-but-so-god-damn arrogant smirk on his lips? Does he see my hands wrapped around my steering wheel, my knuckles white from clutching it so tightly? Can he see my mouth moving as I coax myself into this, the dread seeping into my bones?

If he is, the bastard is probably enjoying it.

I grit my teeth and smooth my expression to one of calm. Big house, flashy car … He's the type of man to enjoy a woman who fawns over his wealth. I will not give him that satisfaction.

Then again, what if *not* giving him that comes at a cost? I only agreed to this for my father's sake. If I don't give Gabriel everything he's wanting or expecting, will he send me packing tomorrow and remove whatever shield he's putting in place to protect my father? That's assuming he's even doing anything to help my father right now. What does his "protection" entail, and is there an expiration date to it? As in, the second he's finished with using me for his own entertainment?

If I was in my right mind earlier, I would have laid out the terms of this deal before I agreed. I was too frazzled though, after the shock of my dad's situation and my ensuing fainting session. So now I'm left with a potentially shitty lopsided deal and twitchy nerves. But, the fact of the matter is, I don't have any other options. Period.

Gabriel is my only hope, as sad as that is.

The time on my dash reads 7:59 p.m. My heart is pounding in my chest as I climb out of my seat and fish my black duffel bag from my back seat. I hit the door lock before I shut the door. And laugh at myself. As if I have to worry about anyone stealing this piece of shit.

Slowly, I pick my way up the landscaped walkway toward the front door, lined by leggy cacti and flowering shrubs and modern lantern lights, my breathing growing shakier with each step. More than anything else right now, I'm nervous. But I refuse to show Gabriel that. I need to be blasé about it all. Give him nothing. Not fear, not nervousness. Certainly not appreciation. This is just a business deal—my body for my father's safety.

Sliding on an unimpressed mask, I hit the doorbell.

And hold my breath, fighting the urge to tug at my jean shorts.

It's about twenty seconds before heavy footfalls approach from inside. I clench my fists in anticipation. Hell, my palms are sweaty.

A man who *isn't* Gabriel opens the door.

"Uh … hi …," I stammer, my cool façade slipping as I'm caught off guard. I try my best to focus on his face and not on his sculpted torso or the ridges of his abdominal muscles or the deep, delicious vee of his hips. He's wearing black dress pants and nothing else. Even his feet are bare.

A wickedly sensual smirk curls the man's lips and I'm hit with a wave of familiarity. That's Gabriel's smirk. Their eyes are similar too—deep-set and blue, though this guy's aren't quite as dark. His nose is more pronounced than Gabriel's—with a bump on the bridge where it was probably broken in the past—and his sable brown hair is longer and wispy.

"Right on time." Gabriel appears then, stealing my breath for a mere second as he does every time I lay eyes on him. He's dressed much like he was last Sunday at Empire, in black pants and a black button-down, the crisp collar open to expose a sexy, thick neck. "I see you've met my brother."

"Brother?" *Of course. Jesus Christ, there are two of them.*

And my gut tells me this one isn't any more innocent than his sibling.

"Caleb, this is Mercy."

"Mercy …," Caleb murmurs, the sound of my name on his tongue sending a warm shiver through my body.

"She'll be staying with us for the next week or so."

With *us*?

I stifle my groan.

Meanwhile, Caleb's eyebrows arch. His brother obviously didn't tell him that they'd be having a room-mate. If he's opposed to the idea, he says nothing, studying me for another long moment before shooting his brother a wry look and sauntering back into the house, toward a set of stairs, giving me a sublime view of his shapely back.

Gabriel pushes the front door shut. "This is all you brought?" He leans in to slip my bag from my grasp, his fingers grazing mine, his cologne tickling my nostrils. "Tell me you have more clothing than this."

"Tell me you actually believe I'll be here for the full week."

He makes a small harrumph. "Let me give you a tour—"

"That's not necessary." I've managed to find my cool composure again, and I wield it like a honed sword. This is not a friendly visit.

We are not friends.

If my tone bothers him, he doesn't let on. "Suit yourself. Follow me."

I trail him into the palatial house, doing my best to hide any semblance of being impressed by the high ceilings and expensive fixtures. It was all bought and paid for with dirty money. Dollars and tears, heartache and loss, from families like mine.

Does he ever feel guilty about that, I wonder?

"Rosita comes every morning around nine. She's a fantastic cook. Anything you need her to buy, add it to that list and she'll pick it up." He waves at a small built-in desk in the corner of a stunning white-and-stainless steel kitchen. "She'll do your laundry and dry cleaning, too, if you leave it in the basket outside the bathroom door."

I let a derisive chuckle out. *Seriously,* how long does he think this ridiculous little game of his is going to last?

"Something funny?"

"No." Tension cords along my shoulders. Nothing about my shit show of a life is funny.

"This way." He leads me down a long hallway, one wall made entirely of windows.

My feet stall as I take in the view—of an expansive patio fit for a hotel, with a stunning round pool that overlooks the valley and the glowing grid of lights from the city below. Phoenix has never looked so alluring to me, but I've never seen it from this angle.

"You're welcome to use it," Gabriel offers with a knowing smile.

I school my expression and continue on, my hard gaze now on his broad shoulders, on the ease of his movements, on the way his tailored pants hug his firm ass.

"Caleb's wing is on the other side of the house," Gabriel says, turning down another hall lined with doors. He leads me through the last one on the right and into a sizeable bedroom with a king-sized bed in the center dressed in crisp white linens.

The air smells like his spicy cologne. I note the half-filled glass of water that sits on the bedside table and the closet to the right, filled with neatly hanging suits, and the shiny watch that sits haphazardly on a small brass table by the door, next to a money clip, the wad of bills impressive.

This is Gabriel's bedroom.

But I always knew this is where I'd end up, I remind myself. All those other doors no doubt lead to other bedrooms—unused bedrooms—but I am staying in *here*. With him.

Swallowing my nerves, I wander over to the wall of windows that overlooks another patio. Gabriel lives in a house of glass and patios.

And pools, apparently.

"*Two* pools?" I blurt out before I can help myself, admiring the long, narrow rectangular shape that disappears around the corner.

"That's a lap pool. You should try it out."

"I didn't bring a bathing suit," I mutter absently. A bathing suit signifies enjoyment, relaxation. I will get neither under this roof.

"You don't need one here."

I let out an unattractive snort. "Right."

"Fine. Check the hallway closet. Rosita's always finding bikinis lying around."

"*Lying around?*"

He shrugs. "Wherever our guests happened to remove them."

"*Guests?*"

"Do you always echo what people say?"

"No. I just find it funny that you call your whores guests. And as if I'm going to wear one of their bikinis." My face twists with disgust.

"Women aren't whores just because they like to fuck. I wish you'd get that out of that gorgeous head of yours." He sets my duffel bag on the floor. "Maybe you wouldn't be so frigid."

I don't know what irritates me more—his words or his casual tone. "Just because a woman doesn't want *you* doesn't mean she's frigid," I snap.

"Frigid *and* a terrible liar." He makes a tsking sound. "What have I gotten myself into?"

"Still time to get yourself out of it."

He eases onto the end of his bed. "Like I told you … I love a good challenge."

I grit my teeth as silence fills the bedroom then, growing thicker with each second that passes.

Finally, I gather my courage. "We need to discuss terms."

"Terms," he repeats lightly. His lips curve with amusement. "Please. Continue."

I take a deep breath. "You wanted me here. I'm here. Now what?"

He stretches his arms behind him and leans back, his hands against the mattress propping him up into a sexy, relaxed pose, his muscular thighs falling apart, his shirt pulling tight against his padded chest.

I hold my breath, my anxiety building as I wait for him to list his demands. Demands that will no doubt be appalling. But he doesn't answer me. He just sits there, those stormy blue eyes boring into my face.

It's unnerving.

So I decide to focus on what *I* need out of this. "What about my father?"

"What about him? He's in the infirmary."

"And when they let him out? How are you going to protect him?"

"He's safe."

"But what if—"

"No one is going to touch him again," Gabriel assures me, his voice overly calm, as if he doesn't tolerate being questioned.

I swallow hard. "Never again? Or just for the next week?" Will my father be tossed to the wolves as soon as Gabriel finds another plaything to amuse himself with?

His gaze drifts downward, like fingers dragging along my skin, over my tank top, my shorts, my legs. "No one's going to attack him again over Fleet. I give you my word," he says. "And before you question that, my word is my bond."

"How very mobster," I let slip, sizing up his bedroom again. The palette is serene, the décor minimalist. Void of personality.

Much like him.

He cocks his head. "What was that?"

"Nothing." I turn my back to him to focus on the lap pool and beyond, but mainly so he can't see how he rattles me. "I want to sleep in one of the other bedrooms—"

He cuts me off with a firm, "No."

I grit my teeth. "Why not?"

"Because that's not part of the deal, and you knew that coming here, so don't try to change the rules. I doubt you'd want me changing the rules on you." He adds after a moment, "Plus, what pleasure do *I* get in that?"

"Sleeping next to a woman who hates you gets you off? Are you that hard up?"

"You don't hate me."

I laugh bitterly. "You're delusional."

"Well … you might hate me," he amends, "but you also want me."

"Are you always this arrogant?" I fire back, though my cheeks burn. I hate that I'm physically attracted to this reprobate. It's worse that he knows it. *Why* am I attracted to him? Why does my body keep betraying me so? Why do I find myself wondering what he looks like naked, what he'll feel like when he pushes into me? It must be a coping mechanism.

There is something seriously wrong with my mental state right now.

"I'm always this right. You'll see. Those dirty thoughts you keep trying not to have about me? You'll eventually give in to them."

"Or I'll just do something horrible to you in your sleep,"

"No, you won't. You're not stupid." The humor in his voice has dimmed. And it's enough of a warning.

He's right, I won't lay a hard hand on him. I'll put up with his taunts and whatever this is, and hope that I come out on the other side for the better.

But I need to gain some level of control.

I need to rewrite this messed-up arrangement to one where I feel like I have some *semblance* of the upper hand.

I dare peer over my shoulder at him. Fair enough, Gabriel is the most attractive man I've ever laid eyes on—personality and criminality aside. So why shouldn't I find some use for him? Why shouldn't I use him while in this predicament? In some twisted way, that idea makes me feel better, more confident.

Less vulnerable.

I've never been one to procrastinate. If there's an assignment I don't want to complete, I do it right away. If I'm dreading hours of errands, I set an alarm and get up extra early to get them out of the way.

If I know I'm going to end up sleeping with a guy in the next week, I may as well just do it on day one.

Oh, wait, I haven't been in this situation before, I remind myself with a grumble.

If there's one thing I know, it's that no guy—no matter how arrogant he is—can resist a naked woman who makes herself available. And the sooner I do that, the sooner we screw, the sooner he realizes that whatever fucked-up fantasy he's feeding off in his head isn't anywhere near the reality, the sooner he'll let me go, the sooner this messed up arrangement will end.

I release a shaky breath.

And then I steel my spine and kick off my sandals.

Collecting the hem of my tank top, I drag it upward, peeling it over my head and off my body, exposing the white lace bra beneath. I keep my back to him and my gaze on the view of the calming water outside as I pop the button on my shorts and drag the zipper down. My heart hammers against my chest but I keep going, letting them fall to the cool tile, stepping out of them daintily.

The slightest hitch of Gabriel's breath sounds in the quiet room. I don't have to face him to feel his burning gaze as he peruses my body, clad in nothing but my bra and panties and flushed despite the chilly conditioned air and the gooseflesh springing over my skin.

I should have asked for a stiff drink from that teak bar we passed, I silently admonish myself as I reach behind me, unfastening my bra. The tension releases, the soft lace cups falling from my body, exposing my breasts. My nipples have beaded; from the cold or my nerves, I can't be sure.

I slip my thumbs beneath my panties on either side, pausing against my hips as I hesitate for a few beats.

Will Gabriel fuck me hard or soft?

Slow or fast?

From behind or while looking down on me?

He did promise me that he would never hurt me, and for some odd, unexplainable reason, I believe him. Maybe that's why I feel confident enough to do this in the first place.

Taking a deep breath—*you are in control now, Mercy; you are using him*—I lift the elastic, letting the cotton drop to pool at my ankles.

He hasn't uttered a word.

And I'm still struggling to find the nerve to meet his gaze. But I can't avoid it anymore. Slowly turning, I find him in the exact same pose as I left him. Only, his lips are parted and his eyes are shining with intention.

And the outline of a hard, long ridge next to his zipper is impossible to miss.

Despite everything, my body begins to respond to the desire in his, the ache forming between my legs.

With measured steps, I approach the side of the bed. I climb on and settle into the center, resting my back against the headboard. I bend and part my legs, just enough to appear sexy, not wanton.

And I wait for Gabriel to turn around, to acknowledge me.

He doesn't move at first.

And when he does, it's painfully slow, easing himself off the end of the bed, his hands going to his rolled sleeves, absently adjusting his cuffs as he rounds the bed with unhurried steps.

I yelp as strong hands seize my ankles and drag my body over, leaving me sprawled out in an ungraceful fashion.

"I thought you said you wouldn't fake it."

"Who says I'm faking it?" My voice is too shaky to sell that lie.

His calloused hands smooth up my calves to my knees, looping around to the backs. He pulls and my body is sliding farther, this time to the edge of the mattress, my hair fanning out, my legs flopping over the side awkwardly. He opens his mouth to speak but hesitates, looming there, his unreadable eyes locked on mine. "This isn't you."

"Don't pretend that you know me or care to," I growl.

"Maybe not. But I only fuck women who *want* it, Mercy." He actually sounds annoyed.

"And didn't you just finish telling me that I wanted you?" I struggle to stifle the sneer. "Well, here I am … wanting you." As much as I hate to admit it, stripping under his watchful eye, lying naked on the bed before him, being handled by his rough hands, having his steady gaze on me, his warm hands gripping my legs, his hard body hovering …

It's causing a strong, heady reaction in my body. Not one I welcome, but all the same, the tawdriness of all this has turned my breathing ragged and made my blood race, and is sending a tingly warmth to my lower belly.

At this moment in time, the idea of watching Gabriel unbuckle his pants is turning me on. If I can just push aside what I hate about him—which is basically everything except his beautiful physical form—I *might* even enjoy this. Or at least pretend to, to his satisfaction. And then I can go home and my father will be safe.

Gabriel lets out a wicked chuckle, his eyes flaring with heat and mischief. "I don't believe you."

I hesitate, but then coax my legs up until my heels touch the edge of the mattress. I part my thighs before him.

His stormy eyes drop, over my bare breasts, over my

flat stomach, to my smooth exposed flesh, where they sit for five … six … seven seconds. He may as well run a finger through my sex, that stare is so intense. My body tenses in response.

A soft hiss escapes Gabriel's parted lips. He kneels between my legs and settles his hands on either side of my head. His muscular body—still fully dressed—hovers over me. His blazing eyes are an inferno of heat and dirty promises as they skate over my eyes, my nose, my mouth.

He leans in, and his thighs force mine to open wider. I grit my teeth against the gasp that threatens as the soft material of his shirt grazes my pebbled nipples, until his lips are an inch away from mine, the body heat radiating off him warming my skin. His minty breath skates over my mouth with each exhale. "Well, you're definitely wet for me," he whispers, and he may as well have pushed his fingers inside me, as intimate as he sounds. "But do you take me for a fool?"

"No?" It comes out like a question.

He shifts, his mouth finding my ear, where he lingers in silence for several long beats, his breathing ragged.

And Christ, I may hate this guy, but the heat pooling between my legs in anticipation of his first touch is next-level. My pelvis rolls of its own accord as my disloyal body eagerly awaits Gabriel's strong hands gripping my flesh.

"Mercy …" He meets my gaze, his full, soft lips brushing against mine ever so lightly. I find mine parting in eagerness. "I'll take you when you're ready to *beg* me for it."

Son of a bitch. "Then I guess you'll be waiting a long time, because I will *never* beg you for it."

His chuckle sends shivers through my body. "We'll see." And suddenly he's gone, the mattress lifting with the loss of his weight. He heads for the door. "Make yourself comfortable. Use the pools, the gym, the kitchen, the bar. Help yourself to anything you want. I should be back around one."

What? "You're *leaving*?" I just offered myself up on a dirty sex platter and he's snubbing me? I pull my legs closed and sit up, acutely aware of how naked and vulnerable I am, even more so than just moments ago.

He collects his watch and money clip. "You have my number on that card if you need it."

That fleeting sexual charge of moments ago has been doused by a torrential downpour of shame and anger. I pull a pillow close to my chest, hugging it as my cheeks burn. "Why are you doing this to me?"

"*To* you?" Gabriel pauses at the door, his eyebrows arched as if he's genuinely surprised by my question. "I'm offering your father protection, and I'm *not* treating you like a whore. Isn't that what you wanted?"

"Fuck you," I hiss. I just spread my legs for him like one.

"Maybe later. We'll see if I'm in the mood." With one last arrogant smile, he strolls out.

My eyes burn with unshed tears. I hate him!

But I hate myself more for succumbing to that brief moment of insanity. There will be no repeat, I promise myself. There is no way I'm ever letting that asshole inside me.

So I guess the next week will be interesting.

He said he'd be back by one. I check the clock on the nightstand.

That gives me almost five hours to get so blind drunk that I can pass out before his return.

16 GABRIEL

I KNEW there was a good reason for our jacked-up home security system.

I watch on our office's computer monitor as Mercy dips her toes into the pool off the living room, balancing a martini glass in her grasp. The stringy black bikini she fished out from the hall closet hugs those intoxicating curves of hers like it was custom made for that perfect body.

I didn't miss the look on her face when I left her in my room, naked and rejected. It was part devastation, part disbelief, part rip-my-face-off feral. I spent the drive to Empire wondering if she'd curl up into a ball in the bedroom and cry the entire time I was gone. That would mean that I'm off my game and entirely wrong about her.

I hoped that her stubborn, defiant streak wouldn't allow it, once she got over herself and the embarrassment of failing at whatever game she was trying to get me to play.

What she didn't seem to realize was that a) my dick was straining against the seam of my pants, and b) I was seconds from whipping it out and shoving it into her pussy. Her tight, smooth, welcoming pussy. There is no mistaking what I saw—Mercy was aroused.

It took Hulk-level control for me to walk away from her.

I jerked in my car the second the engine was humming. Even with a wad of tissues at the ready, I got cum on my goddamn steering wheel. And now here I am, spying on her from the comfort of my office chair and sporting another rock-hard erection. I'm like a prepubescent who just discovered all the wonders of his dick.

"So let me get this straight." Caleb adjusts his tie in the full-length mirror that hangs on the back of our private restroom door—he insists on wearing ties at the club, and he's fucking *obsessed* with having them perfect. "You're making that woman fuck you in exchange for Chops putting the threat of a beat down on anyone who looks twice at her old man? You are one twisted son of a bitch."

"I'm not *making* her fuck me." Hence the jerking session in my car. And the second one that's going to need to happen before I leave this office.

"So you're saying she wants it?" He chuckles. "Because, no offense, bro, but she looked like she wanted to impale your balls with a skewer and roast them over an open flame."

No shit. We have a regular parade of women marching through our doors, and every last one of them fawns over our humble abode and us. Mercy is the first woman who looked utterly apathetic walking through our front door. Though there was that brief moment when she saw the pools and her eyes lit up. It was a beautiful thing. And then it was back to that sucking-on-broken-glass expression. "Not yet. But she will eventually."

"*Eventually*."

"Yeah. Right now, she hates my guts."

Caleb's grin just keeps growing. He's loving this. This whole working-to-get-a-woman thing is a foreign concept to him. Neither of us have ever chased after anyone. We've never needed to. "But making her sit by the pool and watch you ride Lulu or Raina or some other chick is gonna magically win her over."

"Of course not, dumbass. As if I'd do that in front of her."

He pauses with the tie-fussing to shoot me a knowing look. "You've got her *living* with us, Gabe. How's that gonna work out, exactly? You're not discreet."

I flip to another camera, one that gives me a side angle of Mercy downing the rest of her martini in one gulp. She sets the empty glass down and wades to the far edge of the pool, a cliff that's built up by a retaining wall underneath. The view of the city is like nowhere else. Does she have any clue that she's on camera and that I'm watching her? Does she care?

"Gabriel—"

"They're not doing it for me lately. I'm taking a break." Mercy isn't like the usual women we bring home, the kind who will pout when I fuck her friend on

Friday but is all smiles on Saturday, eager to unleash her charmed pussy on me with fervor, convinced that it has the power to turn me into a love-sick monogamous man.

Caleb yanks at the knot in his tie to loosen it so he can start over. "Well, they're doing it for me, so don't think about telling me to rein it in."

"Wouldn't dream of it." I smirk around a sip of my drink. Mercy thinks I'm a pig? Can't wait to see the look on her face when she witnesses one of Caleb's fuck fests. Doubt she'll be ogling his shirtless body like she did tonight ever again after she sees him in full primal action.

"What are we going to do about this *request* you got today?" Caleb asks, suddenly turning the conversation serious, to our father and my visit to Fulcort earlier. Even though we regularly sweep Empire for bugs, we make it a habit to never talk about that side of the business in here—or anywhere where the walls may have eyes and ears.

I shake my head. "Don't know, but we're not getting in bed with *them*." I doubt I could stand in the same room as Camillo Perri or any of his four sons and *not* pull the trigger on my Glock.

"Wonder what the others would have to say about this." The others being Uncle Peter and our two cousins, Alexei and Vic.

I snort. "They'd tell him to go to hell." It seems they're already angling to cut my father out of the business altogether, so why would they heed his demands?

"Maybe not." His reflection catches my gaze and he shoots me a knowing look. "Given our last visit."

"They don't have the same issues that we do," I warn, catching on. The Perri family didn't kill Aunt Rita. She's still drinking her four o'clock cocktails and getting her skin stretched across her cheeks and pretending Uncle Peter doesn't have three side pieces at any given time. She's still there to disapprove of any females our cousins bring home.

Our mother? She wasn't so lucky.

But business is business and if the cartel is making a move, business is in trouble.

"So maybe we pay them another visit and float the idea. Let them run with it. They can dig their own graves."

"Not while we"—Caleb swirls a finger in the air, indicating Empire—"are still tied to it. Otherwise we'll end up in that grave with them." This place has cleaned five times more cash than Uncle Peter's deli and dry-cleaning businesses and Vic's seedy strip club combined. Dad's numerous rental halls did a decent job, but the Feds seized those when they busted him.

"Then we need to make some changes and soon, big brother." Get out of this dirty business altogether.

Caleb chuckles. "Who do you think he'll put a hit on first? You or me?"

"Two-for-one special?" I joke, though it's not funny. We've always done what our father asked of us. He's not the kind of guy anyone defies. But we were also living in this delusional world where we were untouchable.

Who the hell knows how he'll respond when he realizes his sons are no longer interested in the family business?

With one last tug of his tie and a heavy sigh, Caleb mutters, "I'll go do the rounds. Kiss some ass."

"It's what you're good at." Empire caters to serious high rollers, and we do our best to keep them coming back. Some are family business partners. Some are investors wanting to go into business with Caleb and me. Others are socialites and celebrities who boost our club's profile in ways we couldn't buy if we tried.

All of them love Caleb.

"Do me a favor. Ask VIP Four for more discretion," I warn, checking the club's camera feed in time to see a woman snort a line of coke off another woman's lap, right out in the open. We do our best to spot potential undercovers and keep them out, but it's not foolproof. We have high-end restroom facilities in here if they want to be doing that.

A knock sounds on the door, followed by a barely audible female voice, her words muffled by the pounding music in the club.

Caleb opens the door to greet Lulu, dressed in a skintight black bodysuit, her blond ponytail high and tight, her eyes masked with heavy makeup, her skin glistening with perspiration. "You're done early tonight," he says, checking his watch.

"Hey," she drags out softly, through breathless pants. "Yeah, I'm gonna work the floor a bit. Had to finish my shift in the cage a bit early." She presses a hand against her rib cage. "Had a cramp."

Caleb gives her his signature crooked smile, the one that pops those deep dimples women seem to get caught on. We both inherited them from our mother, but Caleb wields them more freely than I do. "How is it down there tonight?"

"Hot." She peels the spandex away from her hard body. "I'm all sweaty."

"I can see that." His gaze trails her hand, stalling at her fake double D tits. "You need the shower?"

She holds up a skimpy red outfit, a coy look on her face. "If you don't mind. No one wants a sweaty shooter girl."

I'd beg to differ. Lulu is sex on heels. Most of those guys out there would gladly lick the salt right off her creamy-skinned body. But that's not why Lulu comes up here to shower. She wants to use our shower because it's more private than the staff change room. And, at her request, it comes with a bonus dick. Two, if she's feeling especially frisky.

Caleb eases back, gesturing her toward the closed door. "Be our guest."

"Hey, Gabe."

"Hey, Lulu."

She winks at me on her way past, swinging those hips of hers suggestively. Lulu spends two hours a day at the gym, and half of that is doing squats. You could bounce a dime off that hard, round ass.

And three ... two ...

"Caleb? Could you help me with my zipper?" she asks sweetly, pausing at the bathroom door to bat her long salon-purchased eyelashes at him.

There's no fucking zipper on that outfit and everyone in this office knows that.

Caleb smirks. "Sure thing, Lulu." He loosens his tie

enough that he can slip it over his head. He tosses it onto the black leather couch in the corner.

"Guess I'm doing the rounds?"

"Thanks, bro." He shuts the door just as the shower begins running.

I sigh, panning back to our home security feed to steal another quick peek at Mercy as she climbs out of the pool, rivulets of water streaming down her slender torso and long legs. My dick swells with excitement. What I wouldn't do to run my hands over her wet skin right now.

She leans over to collect the empty martini glass, stumbling a few steps before correcting herself. How much has she had to drink? And did she go for one of the pricier bottles on the shelf or a cheap bar well stuff? I hope that's a vodka martini and that she went for Caleb's favorite brand. I *really* hope she did it out of spite.

I smile at the thought of a drunk, pissed-off Mercy. That confrontation would be interesting. Will she try to slap me again? I'll be ready for it this time, at least.

Flopping into the lounge chair, she reaches for the silver shaker sitting on the table and refills her glass. I guess that answers my question regarding the booze. She grabs her phone and dials someone. Likely that blond smoke show she came to Empire with last weekend. They seemed tight enough to share their dark secrets. I wonder how she's explaining her current situation. If she's giving details about how she offered herself up and I turned her down.

I wish we had audio on our system.

Mercy stretches her long, sexy body out onto the chair as she talks, her legs swaying casually. She doesn't bother with a towel. There's no need. Nights in July are so hot, you're dry within seconds.

A broad smile stretches her lips, much like it did that first day she was with her father in the visitor room. She has a stunning smile. Unfortunately, I hardly ever get to see it.

I want to see it aimed at me.

A flash of earlier hits me, of a demure Mercy peeling her clothes off, of her climbing up onto the bed, of her parting her legs in front of me, the musky smell of her arousal teasing my senses. Physically, in that moment, she wanted me. That, I'm sure of.

I also know she was trying to give me what she *thinks* I want. She figures I'll get bored and consider her debt to me paid. But I don't want an unwilling woman beneath me. I don't want to just fuck Mercy like I would any of these other women who offer themselves up, legs spread and ready.

I want her eyes on fire as they take me in. I want those plump lips teasing me with promises. I want her on her knees, begging me to ease the ache I've caused deep inside her. I want her unable to think of anything —or anyone—else.

I want her to realize I'm not whatever villain she has decided I am because of my family. I know that's the real problem here. And, yeah, I'm well aware that I haven't exactly helped ease those thoughts with this warped arrangement I've backed her into. I'm just riding on the bet that it won't forever convict me in her eyes. That she'll see I'm not *all* bad.

I sigh, rubbing the bridge of my nose. Sometimes I really am a dumb fuck.

Mercy laughs at whatever the person on the phone said, her fingers absently going to her bikini top, sliding beneath the cup to gingerly scratch an itch. She has beautiful *real* breasts, with small, round pink nipples that were begging to be sucked earlier.

"What have you gotten yourself into, Gabe," I mutter. That woman is going to be in my bed tonight and I'm *not* going to touch her?

Just as quickly, as if realizing what she's doing, she pulls her hand away and her dark eyes slide over the house, searching …

They lock on the camera that I'm watching from and suddenly we're staring at each other. Her gaze narrows suspiciously.

My balls tighten in anticipation just as the first cries behind the bathroom door sound. Lulu is incapable of being quiet. Soon Caleb's deep moans join in, and even the steady thrum of beats from the club can't drown the two of them out.

I grit my teeth in frustration and hit the key to disconnect the security feed before I do something like jerk off while spying on her. I may be a twisted fuck, but I'm not creepy.

I have another two hours before I can head home. To what exactly, I'm not sure yet.

I haul my tense body out of my chair and head for the floor, locking the office door behind me.

17 MERCY

"WHAT'S HIS HOUSE LIKE?" Michelle's voice is an excited hush.

"Pretty much what you'd expect it to be." I take a sip of my vodka martini, savoring the smooth flavor. Gabriel did say to help myself to anything. The fancy crystal-and-gold bottle on the shelf behind the bar looked too enticing not to dip into. And if I wasn't supposed to?

Well, fuck Gabriel. He should have been more clear.

I spent the first hour after he left in misery, wrapped in a fresh terry cloth robe I found hanging on the back of the bathroom door. And then I reminded myself that my father is lying broken in a prison hospital bed and I'm in a mountaintop palace with carte blanche. Not necessarily my freedom at the moment, but it's a hell of a lot more than my dad has.

So I stopped feeling sorry for myself and allowed my simmering rage to take over.

And suddenly things didn't seem so awful.

I found a semi-respectable clean bikini in a pile of raunchy ones—how do all these women forget their bathing suits here? Is it a ploy, an excuse for a return trip to the house after Gabriel or his brother have bedded them? Or are they all just that stupid?—and ventured out here to make the most of a shitty situation by enjoying the stunning view and warm night.

And now I'm getting pleasantly pissed, with two more hours in which to drink enough that I pass out and can avoid whatever Gabriel has planned for when he comes home. That or not remember it.

Maybe this will all go better if I keep myself pickled for the duration of my prison sentence.

"This is *so* crazy, Mercy!" Michelle exclaims.

"I know." I phoned her as soon as I got home from Fulcort earlier today to tell her the situation, pass along Gabriel's address and contact info, *just in case,* and ask her to convince me not to come here.

And she did try. I'll give her a C plus for effort level. She kept getting hung up on how hot Gabriel is and how he could be a sweaty troll, in which case this would be a million times worse. In the end, all I had to think about was my father, and every risk she flagged went out my cracked apartment window. If I can protect my father by whoring myself to Gabriel, then whoring I will do. What I will not do, however, is spread myself wide for him like that again.

I will certainly never beg him to fuck me.

So, if he wants me, he'll have to make his move.

What a sordid, depraved situation I've found myself in.

"Maybe I should pay a visit up to your sex den," Michelle says in a playful tone.

"Nothing has happened yet." And I'm too mortified to admit to what happened earlier.

"What's his brother like? Is he hot, too?"

"It's like they robbed a gene pool." I snort, thinking back to that lumbering old man in orange at Fulcort. Who knew he'd produce such gorgeous offspring? They must take after their mother. Who is their mother anyway?

And where is she while her husband rots in Fulcort?

"I *definitely* have to pay a trip up to Camelback soon then."

"Casting Dean aside already?" I laugh, slipping my fingers into my bikini top to scratch an itch against my nipple.

The cameras.

I yank my hand out quickly, searching the corners of the house. There's one right there, no more than ten feet away and angled directly at me. Of course there is. This place has more cameras than Michelle's family's jewelry store.

Who monitors them? I noticed one inside the front door. Inside the house. I haven't seen any others inside, but for all I know, that shameless display in Gabriel's bedroom earlier was captured.

My stomach twists with horror at that thought.

"... drunk that first night because, I don't know, he just seems sort of vanilla." Michelle's chattering in my ear, pulling me back in. "Especially next to your dark and stormy criminal."

"He *is* actually a criminal, Michelle," I remind her with a sigh. "There's nothing sexy about that."

"Ugh! You're right. But he's being decent so far?"

"So far … I guess." *I'm offering your father protection, and I'm not treating you like a whore. Isn't that what you wanted?* Gabriel's words echo in my mind. He didn't ask me to strip for him. He didn't ask me to climb onto his bed, naked. But he also didn't stop me from doing it. Does he actually see himself as the good guy here?

Michelle and I talk for another half hour—she makes me laugh with her asinine ideas about how to seduce him—until my phone chirps, warning of a low battery. "I should go. My glass is empty and he'll be home soon." I can hear the slur in my words. *Achievement unlocked.*

Time to do a face flop into that big bed.

———

I CRACK my eyelids open and focus on the dim light ahead. Full floor-to-ceiling shades block the sunlight beyond the wall of glass but don't completely obscure the view out from—

I'm in Gabriel's bedroom.

That reality is a jarring blow to my foggy senses as I frantically pick through my memory of last night. After I ended my call with Michelle, I downed one more martini and then stumbled here to shuck my bikini in exchange for my pajamas. The room started to spin, so I crawled into bed and—

A deep, sleepy sigh sounds from the other side of the bed.

My body stiffens as my heart begins racing inside my chest. I assume that's Gabriel, but I don't want to roll over to confirm it; I don't want to risk waking him.

A tall glass of water sits on the bedside table next to two pill bottles—Advil and Tylenol. That was … considerate of him, especially since I have a horrible case of cotton mouth and my head is pounding. Not nearly as hard as I expected it to be though, given I was throwing those vodkas back like a heartbroken cowboy on a three-day bender.

"How much longer are you going to pretend to be asleep?" Gabriel's deep, grating morning voice breaks the silence.

With a reluctant sigh, I reach for the Advil.

"You snore."

"I do not," I deny, my cheeks burning as I struggle to pop the cap off the bottle. Does snoring turn him off? *God, I hope so.*

"Here. Give it to me," he demands after a few minutes of me struggling with the cap.

"I'm fine." I'm not fine. I can't find the strength to lift my head, let alone the coordination to line up these arrows.

The mattress sinks behind me. I feel his body heat against my back—but not his body—as his shapely arm reaches over to rest against my shoulder. He holds his hand out, palm up, waiting. "Stop being stubborn. That rattling sound is annoying."

Fine. I thrust it into his grasp and watch his thumb

turn and pop the cap off with ease, offering nothing more than a grumble of "thanks," when I collect it and fish out two pills.

Thankfully the mattress shifts again, indicating he's moved back to his side. "You were out cold when I got home."

Did he try anything on me? Would he be that big a creep? I steal a glance down at my tank top and boxers. They're disheveled, but nothing beyond the usual after a night of sleep.

"My brother's not happy with you right now. That bottle of vodka that you nearly polished off was just delivered the other day. He likes to have a glass when he gets home after work."

"There's some left." I reach for my water. A dribble. Maybe. "It's not like you don't have other options." That bar stock would rival any nightclub's.

"He's picky. That's why he's willing to pay thirty-eight grand for his vodka."

I choke on a mouthful of water and spend the next few minutes coughing it up. A thirty-eight-thousand-dollar bottle of vodka? I knew it'd be expensive. In my mind, that meant six or seven hundred bucks.

Who the hell spends that kind of money on a bottle of booze?

Gabriel's asshole brother, that's who.

"Good thing he can afford it then," I manage in a strangled voice, chugging the rest of my water in an attempt to rehydrate myself. I'll need at least ten more.

"Are you going to turn around and face me anytime soon?" There's humor in his tone.

"Not if I can help it," I mutter under my breath, falling back into my pillow, my gaze on the lap pool beyond the blinds. It's going to be another hot, sunny day. Any other situation and this would feel like a dream getaway weekend.

"Hmmm."

I can't read meaning into that sound, though I assume it means he heard me.

I reach for my phone to find a string of text messages.

Michelle: Hey, Mercy. How are you? Still alive? He didn't murder you yet?

Michelle: That was a bad joke

Michelle: You're okay, right?

Michelle: Text me when you get up.

It's just after ten. Normally I would have been up hours ago, if I hadn't pickled myself with a vodka bottle worth more than most basic cars. I stifle the vindictive laugh that threatens to escape as I shoot back:

Mercy: I'm fine. Not murdered or molested. Hung over AF.

"I need your work and school schedule," Gabriel says suddenly.

"Why?"

"So I know when you're coming and going. For security."

Something tells me it has nothing to do with security. Is he going to try to control my life? Keep me trapped in here? Unease slips down my spine. "Well, that's easy. I work Monday to Friday from eight until five. I have classes Monday and Wednesday nights from six to nine.

I volunteer Thursday nights, and I go to Fulcort every Saturday." And I plan on studying for the LSAT every other waking moment so I can get my father out of that hellhole.

"Okay."

"Okay?" I echo. "You're not going to try and tell me that I have to stay here?" Impose a curfew on me?

He chuckles. "Seriously, what'd you expect? That I'm going to handcuff you to my bed while I'm out?"

The sheets rustle and my body tenses in anticipation of his hands, of him forcing me to face him. But then the mattress lifts and bare feet slap softly on the tile, moving away from the bed.

I dare steal a glance …

And suck in a breath at a *very* muscular, *very* golden, *very* naked male specimen. Whatever I was imagining in my head about what was beneath those clothes of his, the reality is a thousand times better.

Heat flushes my body as I watch Gabriel stroll for the adjoining bathroom without a hint of modesty, his perfectly round, hard ass cheeks shifting with each casual step. He passes a full-length mirror, and I catch my first glimpse of his cock.

"Holy fuck," I whisper, my already parched mouth going desert-dry. I lay next to *that* all night?

The sound of him emptying his bladder carries— clearly he has no shame—followed by the toilet flushing and the sink tap running, and then he's strolling back into the bedroom, a tall glass of water in his grip.

He's still naked.

Still erect.

Jesus ... The front view of Gabriel is even more impressive, his shoulders bulging, his collarbone cut deeply, his torso rock-hard and padded with ridges of muscle, his thighs powerful ...

His rigid dick long and thick and bobbing with his movements.

As hard as I try, I can't seem to avert my gaze from it, as my face flushes furiously.

He rounds my side of the bed to set the glass next to my empty one, putting his swollen length literally a foot away from my view. He's doing this on purpose, to rattle me. Because how am I supposed to *not* look at it? Close my eyes, I guess.

And yet it's like they're frozen stuck.

That is a pretty penis, I must admit. A fact I'm sure he knows.

"How do you want it?"

"What?" I croak. An ache flares between my legs. *Inside me?*

He wanders off to grab a pair of swim trunks from a hook beside the sliding door, pulls them on, sticking his hand down the front to tuck himself in. "Your coffee. What do you want in it? Milk ... sugar ..." He meets my wide eyes. " ... *cream?*" A devilish smile fills his face and those deep, misleading dimples I caught last week appear. Between that and the fact that his hand is still on his dick, I lose my ability to speak.

So I shake my head in answer.

"Tea, then? Orange juice?"

I finally find my tongue. "No. I drink coffee, just ... no." I tack on a "thanks" at the end. I hadn't heard the original question, too busy gaping at him. And he damn well knew it. This is all a game to him.

"Anything *else* you want to ask me for right now? Anything you *need*?" There's that salacious tone, that wicked, knowing smirk, as he offers to cater to me.

I swallow the flurry of nerves. "Yeah. I need more sleep. Go away."

He studies me, and I have to wonder how frightful my hung over self looks at this moment. "Come out when you've rested. We have a few friends coming over." With that, he leaves the bedroom.

I groan and tug the sheet over my head. I want to punch myself in the face for drooling over him like that.

What the hell is wrong with me?

18 GABRIEL

"Put some fucking clothes on," I grumble, waiting for the Keurig to spit out my coffee. "It's too early in the day to deal with your junk."

Caleb doesn't flinch, leaning back against the kitchen counter with his mug of black coffee, a grin on.

His flaccid dick hanging out.

"Why so grouchy? Your plaything not putting out yet?" he teases.

"All in good time."

"Or maybe she'll take one look at this," he gestures at his groin, "and decide she passed out in the wrong Easton's bed last night."

"Doubt it." Not the way Mercy's mouth was hanging open as she got her first good look at what I have to offer her. She may be hung over and feeling like shit but she is sexy as hell first thing in the morning, with her wild mane of black hair and her dark brown bedroom eyes, and those perfect, pouty lips.

I found her sprawled out on her back when I got

home last night, snoring softly, her cotton tank top riding up, exposing her taut belly. She didn't so much as flinch when I tugged the sheet out from under her limp body to cover her, tucking her in.

Caleb sets his empty mug in the sink and then stretches his arms over his head and releases a loud groan. "It's gonna be a good day." His gaze settles on the main patio, on a topless Lulu as she smooths sunscreen over an equally topless Raina's back. Both of them spent the night in Caleb's bed. My guess is they'll end up back there again before the day's through.

The security alarm dings with the warning that a car just turned into our driveway. It's the first of what will be many. Sundays get busy here and, given we've got management covering Empire tonight, it'll probably also get wild.

"Guess I should cover up," Caleb says reluctantly.

"Thank God." I savor the first sip of black coffee, wondering if Mercy likes hers bitter or sweet or creamy. The look on her face when I dropped that lewd joke made me want to laugh. In my dirty mind I was shooting my load all over her face, her tongue; pulling her top down to come all over her tits. The effect those thoughts had on my cock were priceless.

She couldn't keep her eyes off me.

"Where's your girl? Sleeping off my fucking vodka?"

"Something like that." I grin, remembering the pleasant surprise of finding that empty bottle last night, though my guess is, if she had known what it was worth, she never would have touched it.

He punches keys on his phone's keypad and in

seconds the house's music system is pumping with dance beats. The girls' outside wave their hands in excitement. "So she wouldn't appreciate this, then?" He cranks it up with a wicked smile.

———

"CAN YOU DO ME?"

I was on the verge of drifting off in my shady corner when the seductive female purr pulls me back to consciousness.

There's a split second when I think—hope—that it's Mercy, finally venturing out of my bedroom. But when I open my eyes, I find Raina hovering next to me, topless and waving a bottle of sunscreen in the air, her tits jiggling with the movement.

There have got to be thirty other people milling around our place—lingering in the pool, chilling in the shade with drinks, picking at the pizza in the kitchen—who could do it but of course she comes and wakes my ass up.

With a murmured, "Sure," I slide my legs to either side of my lounge chair, making room for the busty redheaded college student who tends bar at Empire on Fridays and Saturdays.

And has eagerly tended to my dick on many other occasions.

Frankly, she's too young for me—twenty-two, I think?—and on the too-skinny side for my liking. She also goes out of her way to say what she thinks I want to hear.

Not like Mercy, I think with a smile.

Shit. Raina probably thinks that smile is for her.

She settles down between my legs, edging back until her ass is nestled against my balls.

Yup, definitely thought that was for her.

"So, where'd you go last night?" she asks in a pouty voice, shuddering at the first glob of lotion against her skin.

I smooth my hands over her bony shoulders. "To bed. I was tired." And I'm not about to explain the rest my Mercy-situation, to her or anyone.

"Poor baby. You've been working so hard lately." Her fingers skate over my knee.

"Not really." I quickly cover her back. That's the good thing about being this rich—I pay other people to work hard.

"Well … I missed you."

I give her slender shoulders an affectionate squeeze. She may be easy but she's a sweet girl. "All done."

"What about the rest of me?" She leans back to lie on me, her head nuzzled at my neck, her long red hair tickling my face, giving me a great view of her tits.

"You can't handle doing that?"

She giggles. "I'd rather you did. And while you're doing that, I can handle something else." She moves fast, her arm slipping between us, her fist seizing my cock over my shorts.

If Mercy weren't in the picture, this is where I'd let her jack me.

But Mercy *is* in the picture—albeit hiding upstairs, hating me—and this is exactly the kind of shit that won't fly with getting her to come around in her low opinion of me.

"Not today." I reach between us to ease her hand off me, and then gently nudge her up so I can climb off the chair. I head straight for the pool to cool off, the afternoon heat oppressive even in the shade. Also, to kill the semi that Raina stirred because, come on, no breathing guy can't *not* react to that.

"Yo, Gabe," Felix, calls out, wading toward me, trailed by his twin brother, Finn. I've known them since I was thirteen, when a group of punks jumped Caleb and me one day on our way home from school. The twins happened to be walking by, so they threw down in our defense in what ended in a bloody mess. They've been in our circle ever since.

We clasp hands. "Hey, man, didn't see you come in."

"You were indisposed." He chuckles, his gaze flittering over Raina and her perky breasts, before shifting to a spot behind me, in the distance. "Who is *that*?"

I glance over my shoulder and immediately note where his attention has gone—a bikini-clad Mercy is sauntering across the upper deck outside my bedroom, heading toward the lap pool.

She lives.

"A friend."

"Fuck … *Dude*. Introduce me." His golden eyes flare with meaning.

Not a chance. "Hey, how long has she been up there?" How much did she see of the Raina-sunscreen show?

"Dunno. Ten, fifteen minutes? She was fussing with the umbrella for a while."

I sigh. Great. All of it, probably.

This should be interesting.

19 MERCY

WAY TO LIVE up to my expectations, Gabriel.

I hide my watchful gaze behind my dark, oversized sunglasses—perfect for both shielding against the intense, blinding sun and spying on my captor as he rubs down the mostly naked twig with boobs sitting between his legs. That white triangular scrap of material over her crotch may as well not be there.

Apparently, Sunday is party central at Chez Easton Brothers. The calm, peaceful patio that I enjoyed all to myself last night is crawling with hot bodies—runway-model girls and brawny jock guys, drinks in hand, talking, laughing, swimming, milling around, music pumping through the speaker system.

That goddamn music! Gabriel wasn't gone from the bedroom five minutes before it started blasting. At least it wasn't filtering through the speaker in his bedroom ceiling, thank God. My aching head could not have withstood that.

And now the twig is lying back on Gabriel, her

breasts jutting into the air, her arm *mysteriously* disappearing between their bodies. She's going to jack him off right there, out in the open. Would she care that he was lying naked in bed next to another woman just hours ago?

That he's running a twisted bribery scheme to keep said desperate woman there?

Because *he* clearly doesn't.

An odd twinge stirs in my gut. I'm not surprised to see this.

But I think I'm disappointed that I wasn't wrong about him.

A small part of me was wishing that I was.

I avert my gaze and focus on adjusting the massive overhead umbrella that will offer me shade while I work on my assignments—after a quick dip in the pool that hopefully expels the rest of this wretched hangover. Normally I'd be at the library today, huddled in a private cubicle and surrounded by books, the cool air pumping through the vents more refreshing than our apartment. I'll admit, this is far from horrible as an alternative. I'm hungry though, and craving something greasy to soak up the rest of the alcohol lingering in my veins. But finding food would require venturing out *there* and being social.

For now, a swim will have to do the trick.

From the corner of my eye, I note that Gabriel is now in the main pool, his twiggy vixen perched on the chair he left, her mouth downcast as she watches him go. Pouting. Hmm … interesting.

There's no way she got him off that quickly and

discreetly, which means he must have declined her advance.

Why am I feeling a sense of relief over that?

Setting my sunglasses down on the table, I saunter for the lap pool, grateful that it's empty, that the party has remained in the main area and not spilled over this way. I hope it stays that way.

Who the hell has a lap pool? I ask the question again as I study the structure stretching out ahead of me. It's exactly what you'd think it to be given the name. Long and narrow—just enough for one person to get their daily exercise. And it's suspended over the cliff much like the other pool. Insane. I can't imagine what something like this would cost to build.

Oh, the things dirty money can buy.

The sun is blistering hot but the water is refreshingly cool against my skin as I slip under, reveling in the silky clean feel of the salt water caressing my hot scalp, soothing my discomfort.

A soft moan escapes my throat as I surface. I glide over to fold my arms over the concrete edge and admire the view. The mountain is speckled with tall, leggy cacti and mansions much like this one. The ones farther down may be smaller and not quite as luxurious, but they're nice in their own right. I'd take *any* of them.

A sound stirs behind me. I turn to find Gabriel setting a plate and tall glass of water on the patio table.

"It's pizza. Figured you might be hungry," he says by way of greeting, strolling toward the pool, his damp shorts hanging low and clinging to his lower body. The rigid outline of what's hiding beneath is unmistakable.

God, why am I salivating right now?

Because, despite everything, you're still attracted to him, you idiot.

With perfect form, Gabriel dives into the pool, cutting through the water. He surfaces next to me, his broad chest coated with water, his hair slicked back, only accentuating the square cut of his chiseled jaw.

Sharp blue eyes hone in on me.

I turn away and resume my valley-gazing position. I don't want him seeing the lust I'm feeling right now. He saw enough of that earlier today, when his impressive asset was bobbing around.

"Feeling better?" he asks, and his voice has turned low and gravelly.

"Marginally," I admit after a beat.

"You shouldn't have drank so much."

"My current situation called for it," I throw back bitterly.

He answers with a deep chuckle.

The fucking asshole thinks this is funny.

"Come on, Mercy. Admit it, being here isn't as horrible as you thought it'd be."

"Don't you have a redheaded waif waiting with bated breath to give you what you want?"

I tense as he moves into position behind me. His calloused hands settle next to my elbows on either side, his arms closing me in. "That's not what I want." His body presses against mine, sandwiching me between him and the pool wall. I stifle my gasp at the feel of his hard length lined up against the crack of my ass. "That's not *who* I want."

I take a calming breath. "*Right*. Well, since you'll be waiting until hell freezes over, you may as well get it from somewhere else."

"Until hell freezes over ..." he echoes, amused. "You know, that will probably happen, with all this doom-and-gloom climate change."

I grit my teeth against the urge to smile. He's clever, this one. "Not in the next week, it won't."

"Maybe I should change the terms, then." He drags a thumb over my elbow in an affectionate move.

I swallow. He wouldn't, would he? "To what?"

"To long enough for you to change your opinion of me."

Does he really think there's *anything* he can do at this point to change my opinion of him? I bite my tongue against voicing that out loud. He's helping me. If I keep being an outright bitch to him, he might decide he's had enough.

"You better take what you can get elsewhere, or you're going to be suffering horribly this week," I say instead.

I feel so tiny, encased in his arms, as he leans forward, his ripped chest against my back, to float his lips a mere inch from my ear. "Is that what you want? For me to fuck other women while you're here?"

That odd twinge stirs in my stomach again at the thought of him with another woman. I know he's been with scores of them. It's silly to be bothered by it. "Since when does what I want matter to you?"

His deep exhale caresses my wet skin. He doesn't say anything for what feels like forever, before instructing,

"Eat and then get dressed. Meet me outside in twenty minutes."

I frown as wariness sets in. "Why?" Is he releasing me from this perverse arrangement of his? Should I pack?

"Twenty minutes," he repeats, and then he's moving away from me and swimming for the other side, every muscle in his back and shoulders straining as he deftly pulls himself out. "And wear something on the respectable side."

No, he's not letting me go yet.

But I'm intrigued.

———

THE FEW PARTYGOERS lingering inside are so focused on the baseball game playing on the massive flat-screen TV that I manage to duck out the front door without being noticed. The Lambo's already purring in the driveway next to a long line of vehicles tucked neatly along one side of the lane.

A nervous flutter stirs in my stomach as I make my way along the path, discreetly smoothing my hands over the skirt of the floral spaghetti-strap dress I chose from my limited options. I wear it to work often. It's on the shorter side, but it's a nun's habit compared to that silver number I wore to Empire last weekend. To be safe though, I grabbed a soft pink cardigan to throw over.

The passenger-side door does its space-ship style glide open as I approach.

My flat sandals afford me a much more graceful entry this time.

Gabriel's eyes are covered by sunglasses, but I feel that hot gaze sizing me up.

"Is *this* respectable enough for you?" My tone is almost accusatory. He's in his usual jeans and T-shirt.

His lip quirks. "It'll do."

I slide my seat belt on. "Where are we going?"

All I get in answer is that sexy one-sided smirk, and then he cranks the volume on the radio up and we're coasting down the driveway, the vibration of the powerful engine humming through my core.

I sigh, too tired to play whatever this new game is and still feeling the effects of last night's vodka. "Wake me up when we get there." Turning my head away from him, I shut my eyes and pretend to sleep to the steady drone of the baseball commentator.

Until I'm no longer pretending.

Chain-link.

Dumpsters.

Where are we? I wonder as I come to, blinking my eyes repeatedly over my surroundings.

A guard in a beige uniform walks by, and it clicks.

We're at Fulcort.

"Hey, Frankie," Gabriel offers, his deep raspy voice taking on a friendly tone as he talks to the hulking tattooed guard hovering next to our car. He reaches out to shake hands with the man. I don't miss the wad of green bills that gets passed along, though it's too smooth for me to catch any denomination. "All set?"

"Keep your windows down," the guard—Frankie— answers, then nods to someone ahead of us. A loud buzz sounds, and the heavy chain-link fence slowly rolls open.

"What is this?" I take in the high concrete walls and rows of security Jeeps.

"The back way in."

"There's a back way in?"

The engine revs and we begin moving through. "There's *always* a back way, babe."

We coast through a few more checkpoints, heavily armed guards halting us with a hand, poking their heads in to inspect the interior, until we pull up next to an ambulance.

Gabriel cuts the engine as my heart begins pounding. "Is this the infirmary?"

"It's somewhere on this end, yeah." He points to a tall blond guard. "He's going to take you in to see your father."

"I thought it wasn't allowed. It's against prison rules."

"It's not. And it is."

Unless you're Gabriel Easton, who lives by no rules.

Gabriel hits the button to open our doors. I follow his lead and climb out, feeling self-conscious about all the eyes on us as we circumvent the prison system. I wish I'd known we were coming here—I would have worn my usual garb.

Gabriel comes around the car to meet me. "I bought

you ten minutes, fifteen at most. When they say you need to go, you *need* to go, no issues. Okay?"

"Yeah. Okay." My head bobs dumbly. "That's fine."

"And don't say anything about how you got in here, or who helped you," he warns, his hand settling on the small of my back to gently lead me forward. For once, his touch is soothing my nerves, given the tense circumstances. "If your father asks, you tell him it doesn't matter."

I lick my dry lips. "Got it."

The stony-faced blond guard buzzes us in without a word and we trail him down a narrow corridor. There's no sign of inmates or guests here, but I'm guessing this passageway isn't intended for anyone but prison staff. We step into a small nondescript room.

"I've got to search you," the guard announces.

The hairs on the back of my neck stand on end.

"What the fuck, you think she's gonna shank her own father on his sick bed?" Gabriel growls.

"I've seen crazier shit than that," the guard retorts smoothly. "If she wants to wait a few weeks and go through our regular security just like everyone else, she's welcome to."

"No," I rush to say, shooting Gabriel a warning look. "It's okay. I'll … do this." What does this search entail, though? Pervy Parker's dirty promises of strip searches surface, and dread seeps into my bones. But the sooner this is over, the sooner I can see my father, know that he's going to be okay. I seem to be living life by those words lately.

Gabriel's jaw tenses. Folding his arms over his broad

chest, he leans back against the wall. "Surface level only, and I'm staying."

The guard's hard eyes flash to Gabriel. He doesn't like being told what to do. A long moment passes, and then he gives an almost imperceptible nod. "Arms up, legs apart," he commands.

I follow orders and hold my breath as rough hands begin their hunt. The good news is that there aren't many places to conceal anything within this dress. The bad news is that this guard is intent on thoroughly checking the few places there are.

I close my eyes and grit my teeth as his palms land on my breasts, pushing and prodding every inch of flesh, smoothing his fingers back and forth several times along my bra's underwire before he seems satisfied. He's not making me take it off, at least.

The invasive search continues over my stomach and back.

I suck in a breath as his hands slides along the crack of my ass.

"That's good, yeah?" Gabriel asks, but it's not really a question, the cold fury in his eyes as he regards the guard enough to make any man pause.

The guard steps back, a flicker of wariness on his face. "Follow me."

Gabriel's hand settles onto my spine again as the guard leads us down another maze of corridors and secured doors and I try to shake off those few minutes of discomfort.

My nose catches the scent of antiseptic, and a moment later we're stepping into a long room of mostly empty beds. Two have hospital curtains drawn around them, presumably to offer the inmates privacy.

There's no medical staff in here. I have to wonder if that's intentional—don't see, can't talk. No witnesses means no rules have been broken.

"Ten minutes, and keep it quiet." The guard pulls a curtain open, revealing my father.

I gasp and rush forward to gingerly take his limp hand. As bad as his face was when I saw him last, this is a million times worse. He doesn't look like my father.

Not until he cracks his swollen eyelid and I see his soft gray iris. "Mercy," he croaks. "How'd you get in here?"

"It doesn't matter." I fight the tears that threaten to spill, but fail. "How are you feeling?"

"Better. Chest hurts, but ..." He starts shifting, trying to pull himself up, his face pinching.

"Don't! Stay where you are." I ease onto the side of the bed to cradle his hand in both mine. No one's here to bark at me about contact. I need to take full advantage of it while I can. "Tell me you've taken something for the pain?"

"I'll be fine."

"No, you won't, Dad! Take something!" For as long as I can remember, my father has refused any and all pain medication. I know it's on account of my mother's addiction, and it's commendable. Now though, it's downright idiotic.

"They pumped some shit into me at the hospital but around here the options are limited. It's okay though ..." He chuckles, and winces again. "I was begging them to let me back to my cell so I could see you again." Even with his mangled face, he manages a smile. "This is a damn nice surprise."

I brush away my tears and offer a sad smile. "It is, isn't it? I don't know if it'll happen again."

"Well, tell whoever helped you get in here that I said thank you."

I glance over my shoulder. The curtain's closed, but I know Gabriel's out there somewhere. "I will," I find myself murmuring.

20 GABRIEL

Her old man lets out one of those soft chuckles—the kind a person gives when every last breath they take feels like a stab to their chest. In his case, that's probably accurate.

"Hey, Donny." I edge over to the far corner where the short, stocky guard stands. It's a good thing the blond guard vanished, because I was ready to rip his vocal cords out through his throat for the grope fest back there. "What're they giving him?"

"No idea, but nowhere near enough is my guess. Should have stayed in the hospital for another week, but you know how it is. Budget and all that."

"Yeah." Twenty-four-hour guard duty on a hospital room eats up a lot of money every time one of these guys gets jumped with a capital beat down. "Is there anything better that the doc can prescribe him to help?" I give him a knowing look. *Something that isn't readily available and can't end up in any patient charts.*

Donny's green eyes dart to me before shifting straight ahead of him. "Not sure."

"I'd consider it a personal favor." And Donny knows all about those. The GTO he climbs into every day to get here was not paid for with his meager salary.

After another moment, he nods. "I'll do what I can."

"Thank you. Safely, of course." Last thing I need is the guy coding because they slipped him too much Fentanyl or something equally potent.

"Of course." He opens his mouth to say something, but then firmly shuts it, as if thinking better. My guess is he's wondering why I'm bothering with all this.

I'm definitely wondering why I'm bothering.

A few minutes pass, the low murmur behind the curtain constant as Mercy catches up with her father.

And then Donny says, "I heard the guy who did this hanged himself last night."

I affix my gaze to the white concrete wall across the way. "Really."

"Yeah. With a belt."

"Those usually work well."

"They do. They can't figure out how he got it into solitary though. There was a glitch with the security feed last night. Cameras stopped working for about fifteen minutes."

Plenty of time to miss anyone who might have been around the cell with a belt.

"He must have been overwhelmed with guilt over his gangbanging life," I offer solemnly.

Donny studies those same white bricks alongside me. "Yeah. Must have."

A door at the other end of the infirmary creaks open and another guard—Monroe, if I remember correctly—pokes his head in. A warning that the nurse on call is finishing up her administrative meeting—that we arranged as a distraction—and is heading back.

"Sorry, man. Time to go." Donny takes a step toward the sick bed.

"Hey, I've got one more favor to ask."

He sighs, but then nods. "What is it?"

"Chops. He needs a private visit with his hooker tonight." I think the beast is in love.

Donny frowns. "I thought those were only for fight nights."

And special rewards.

"Just fucking set it up." I pull the wad of cash out of my pocket and hold it out for him. I'm bleeding bills for Mercy lately. Not that I can't afford it, but still.

Donny pauses for only a beat before collecting it. "Have her here for eleven."

———

IT'S ALMOST six by the time I'm pulling onto the freeway again. Mercy hasn't said a word since Donny led us out of Fulcort, and now she sits quietly in the passenger seat, her arms roped around her slender waist as if in comfort, her beautiful face drawn.

"I know that was short but … good visit?" I finally ask.

It's a few beats before she gives a single nod. She swallows. "Thank you. For making that happen."

I could say all kinds of things—tease her, ask her to repeat that, wonder out loud how she might want to repay me—but I bite my tongue and ask instead, "How did he end up in there, anyway?"

"I told you already." She studies a chipped nail. "He got into a fight and the other guy died."

"No offense, but he doesn't look like a big threat."

"He's not. Fleet did something, my dad lost it, and … It was a freak accident."

"What'd Fleet do?" I steal a glance to find her chewing her bottom lip, as if considering whether she wants to divulge that. Fuck, she's got the sweetest-looking lips. My dick stirs at the thought of kissing them.

"He had a bit of an obsession with me."

I can understand that, Fleet. I've seen the way the guards and visitors—pretty much everyone—look at Mercy as she walks by. Her face alone grabs attention, whether she wants it or not.

"One day after work, my car wouldn't start. So I left it there and grabbed a ride with someone to school. I came back after class to meet the tow truck from my dad's shop, Billy's Wreckers, out near Tolleson. My dad's been working there for the past fifteen years. Anyway, Fleet was on call that week so he was the one to come out with the truck." Her lips twist up with repulsion. "It was almost ten at night so everyone at Mary's had left. He cornered me in the parking lot and started telling me how he loved me and we were meant to be, and that we belonged together, and all kinds of psycho crap." She shudders. "We had never even talked before that night beyond, like, a polite hello."

"Sometimes that's all it takes for a certain type of guy."

"Yeah, no shit," she mumbles, rolling her eyes. "Anyway, I told him I wasn't interested. I was nice enough about it. But I guess he had no plans on taking no as an answer." Her face is a steely mask as she stares out at the freeway. "He grabbed me. Covered my mouth to keep me from screaming and dragged me into the alleyway behind Mary's."

My fists tighten around my steering wheel. "He's lucky he's already dead."

Her gaze flashes to me before shifting away again. "Thank God it was winter and I was wearing jeans. If I'd been in something like this"—she gestures at her dress—"it would have been harder to stop him. But I managed to fight him off and get away. Luckily I know the security passcode for Mary's, so I hid in there and called the police. He was gone by the time they arrived, but I filed a report. They gave me a ride home and said they were going to pick him up. But they didn't, because he showed up the next day at Billy's." She swallows hard. "My dad lost it on him. Fleet was a lot bigger, but my dad went at him with everything he had. He wasn't thinking straight, he was so angry." She takes a deep breath. "He hit Fleet in the head with a wrench and the guy died."

"A *wrench*?" I've seen a guy get his knuckles broken with a wrench, but to kill a guy ... "He only hit him once?"

"Only once. *Hard*. Caught him just the right way across the temple, apparently. My dad has never hit anyone before, for as long as I've known him. Like I said, it was a freak accident." She smooths her hand over her skirt, tracing the tiny flowers with her fingertip.

"That asshole got what was coming to him. Your dad deserves a medal."

"Yeah, well, he's paying for it with his life instead. The prosecutor said it was premeditated because of what Fleet had done to me. He got twenty-two years because we couldn't afford a decent lawyer to argue against that." Her lip wobbles. She turns away, but not before I see the tears brimming.

I can't help myself. I reach across the console to slip my hand around hers, to give it a comforting squeeze. She doesn't respond immediately, but then her limp hand tightens within mine. It only lasts a moment before she's shaking herself free of my grip and folding her arms over her chest once again.

The freeway is quiet right now, the lanes ahead wide open. As much as I feel the urge to open up the engine on this car and speed, I keep my foot light on the gas pedal. Mercy's already been through enough today.

And, yeah, I'll admit that some of that is *my fault*, with this whole arrangement I've thrust on her.

"I asked the guard to see if he could get your father something to dull the edge. Something better than whatever it is they're giving him now."

"He won't take it."

"If he's in that much pain, he will."

"No." She shakes her head furtively, brushing at her cheek with the back of her hand. "He won't take painkillers of any kind. He'll refuse them."

"Seriously?" I frown. "That's idiotic."

"Not if your wife died of an overdose," she counters, her voice filled with venom suddenly. "Not if you watched the woman you love wither away because she couldn't function without something to dull the edge off life, and you did everything you could to help her but you couldn't stop it because there was always some scumbag waiting around the corner to sell it to her."

And there it is.

The root of why Mercy resents me, even as those dark eyes can't seem to stay off me.

An odd feeling courses through my body as realization hits. She isn't just some self-righteous woman who has decided not to like me because we met at a prison. She's not a hypocrite because she's concocted a delusional story about how her father doesn't deserve to be in prison while mine does—though she'd be right.

She has a legitimate, personal beef.

She thinks *I'm* that scumbag.

"I'm not into dealing drugs, Mercy," I blurt out before I can stop myself.

"Really? So you're saying all this money you have," she casts her delicate hand toward my dashboard, "wasn't made with drugs?"

I grit my teeth. As if I'd ever admit to that. And yet the automatic denial that *should* fall from my lips—that I've sung more than once when sequestered in interrogation rooms with the Feds while they've tried to wrench info from me—won't. "I'm not my father," I say instead, because I'm not. I don't *want* to be.

"Yeah, I thought so," she mutters, then turns away.

"What was it?" I ask. "Your mom."

"Heroin," she whispers after a moment, and her body seems to slump, as if suddenly sapped of energy.

Good ol' Harriet. Shit … "Here in Arizona?"

"No. Virginia. We moved here after she died."

Relief swells inside me. At least it wasn't our product that did her in. "I'm sorry you lost your mother like that."

Mercy bursts out laughing.

Okay, not the reaction I was expecting.

"Please just let me go home, Gabriel," she pleads.

I break from my focus on the road for a moment to meet her gaze. If I were a decent man —a selfless man—I would acquiesce. Hell, I never would have required any of this from her in the first place.

But I can't. Not yet. Not until she sees that I'm not *all* bad.

Without a word, I take the turn-off toward Camelback Mountain.

———

THE LINE of visitor cars has dwindled to three by the time we arrive home.

The passenger door is barely up before Mercy is climbing out. She doesn't acknowledge Caleb's cherryred Porsche or the three other luxury vehicles parked in the garage, her sole focus seemingly to get away from me as fast as possible.

"Mercy, wait up! Before you head in there, you

should probably know ..." My words drift as she storms through the front door, ignoring me.

I can't help my smile as I enter a few seconds after her to find her frozen in place, taking in the view through the glass of Caleb buck naked and laid out on a lounge chair while Raina rides him. Meanwhile, the twins are perched at the edge of the spa, catching the last of the sun while having their dicks spit-polished by Lulu's friends.

"I tried to warn you." I come up behind her. "Things can get wild around here sometimes."

Mercy's jaw is clenched as she takes it all in.

I dare set a hand on the curve of her lower back. Aside from those few moments yesterday when she was naked on my bed, it's the only place I've dared touch her. "You okay?"

"I sat on that chair last night" is all she says after a moment, and then she's marching toward the hall that will lead to my bedroom, her head held high.

21 MERCY

I NEVER THOUGHT I'd find the walls of Gabriel's room a comfort, but as I pull the door shut behind me, my body sags with relief, the weight of the weekend finally hitting me.

I'm beginning to think no amount of sleep will make me feel better. I could crawl into those cool white sheets now and sleep until tomorrow morning and *still* feel like I've been hit by a Mack truck, the driver called Shitty-Ass Life behind the wheel.

But sleep isn't in the cards for me, I accept. I have an assignment due tomorrow night that's going to take me hours to finish.

And then I have Gabriel.

How am I supposed to fall asleep with *him* in bed—likely naked—next to me?

Will he try something tonight? Will he *expect* something in exchange for getting me into the prison to see my father? A kindness that he wasn't obligated to show.

Was it to prove in his twisted way that he does in fact care about what I want? Who knows what that cost him. Not that he can't afford it.

Plus, he was oddly solemn—dare I say, sweet?—today at Fulcort. The Gabriel I assumed he was would have kicked back with a grin while that guard ordered me to strip, but he looked ready to choke the man out the second he laid his hands on me. And his whole demeanor was different this afternoon. Respectable, almost. Well, aside from that moment in the pool, which I'll never admit to him that I enjoyed—but God, did he feel good against me.

He's forcing me to be here, I remind myself. Forcing me to share his bed. But he has yet to force me to do anything more. Will he keep me here for the full week and not eventually demand sexual favors?

And where is my head going to be at after a week of naked Gabriel strutting around, given I've been here one day and already I'm entertaining ideas I don't want to be entertaining?

Maybe I can ask him to put on shorts.

Yeah, because that will make a huge *difference.*

I groan. I can't believe I'm beginning not to trust myself around him!

If this keeps up, I'm going to need to break into the Ambien tonight. It's that or drink myself into oblivion, and that's not an option, not with the long day ahead of me tomorrow.

Tossing my purse onto the nearby dresser, I kick off my shoes and spend a few minutes freshening up in the bathroom. My stomach is grumbling. I caught the scent of grilled meat when we got home, but I never got a chance to find out if it was from Gabriel and Caleb's backyard or somewhere else, thanks to the fuck fest going on outside.

My cheeks flush at the visual now emblazoned in my mind. It's not the first time I've seen people having sex— some of the frat parties I've been to were enlightening, to say the least. Usually it was late in the night, when everyone was stumbling drunk or high. You'd inevitably walk into the kitchen and find some girl on her knees, sucking off her boyfriend, or wander into the games room to see two best friends putting on a show for a group of cheering, horny frat boys.

There'd be whispers the following week, rumors. Sometimes picture evidence. Usually bowed heads and a looming cloud of regret.

But that show out there on the back patio, as the sun was setting over the horizon?

Something about that felt entirely different. Next-level, as Michelle would call it. Sure, they're all likely drunk—they've been drinking all day—but my gut says this is the kind of stuff that happens on the regular here, and none of those girls will feel an ounce of regret for having cycled their way through these guys.

How often has Gabriel been out there with them, fucking girls alongside his brother?

The girl riding Caleb is the redhead who was all over Gabriel earlier. He didn't seem the least bit fazed that she'd moved on.

How many times has she ridden Gabriel like that, poolside?

Is he out there right now, unfastening his pants and waiting his turn?

My gaze darts to the patio table where my books sit, untouched. I *need* my books to do my assignment. But going out there to collect them means witnessing the debauchery.

And confirming if Gabriel has joined in.

If he has, it would mean I've been right about him all along. And if he hasn't …

"Oh my God." My stomach sinks with disappointment and realization sets in. A part of me is desperate to be wrong about Gabriel. There's only one reason for that: I've finally lost my damn mind. My physical attraction to him is taking over all rational thought.

I swallow my unease, and, holding my head up as if I'm unbothered, I slip out the patio door. A woman's high-pitched cries and the sound of skin slapping skin greets me. From the corner of my eye, I spot Caleb, now on his feet, his hands gripping the twiggy redhead's hips as he thrusts into her from behind. *That can't be comfortable.* I watch her struggle to maintain her balance, her legs stretched over the lounge chair, her body propped up by her elbows.

As seedy and depraved as it is to watch, heat stirs between my thighs.

I refocus my attention on collecting my things, but it doesn't last long, as a deep guttural groan sounds from elsewhere. Could that be Gabriel? If it is, he didn't waste any time.

I can't help myself; I need to know.

Hugging my books, I swallow my growing dread and shift to the other side of the table, where I can get a better view of the pool and the spa beside it.

It's not Gabriel, I confirm, as one of the two brawny men—I think they're twins?—cries out, his hand on the back of the blond's head as she blows him. It seems to set the second guy off because he starts thrusting his hips into his girl's mouth, his head falling back as his rigid abdominal muscles tense.

"Hungry?" Gabriel's voice sounds behind me, startling me from my voyeurism.

I spin around, my cheeks flushing.

A smirk curls his lips as he sets a plate down, loaded with a burger and a salad. "Didn't know what you wanted so I put them on the side." He gestures at the dollops of ketchup and mustard.

"Thanks," I offer after a beat. People are fucking on the patio and he was inside, fixing me a burger? The mental image of that almost makes me laugh. But it also means he's not down there, and I am so relieved about that. *Stupid girl.*

He pulls out a chair. "Come on. Sit and eat."

"Oh God, Caleb. Make me come!" Twiggy cries out, bringing our current sordid situation back into focus. Bodies begin to slap harder.

"I can't eat out here with that going on, Gabriel."

"They'll be done in a minute." His lip curls. "My brother never lasts long after a woman says that."

"Wow, you have his sex habits down pat, huh? What a good, kind brother you are." The sarcasm is flowing freely from me now. "I'm surprised you're not down there with them."

His eyebrow arches. "Is that what you want? For me to go down there and fuck one of those women?"

"I don't care what you do."

He sighs as he rounds the table and stops to hover just inches from me, to stare down at me a long moment. He seizes the textbooks I'm holding in my arms, his fingers grazing my skin in the process. Goose bumps erupt all over my body despite the warm air.

"Really?" He drags the pad of his thumb down my arm. "Is that what these are for? Because you *don't* care?"

"I'm cold," I lie.

I get a crooked, dimpled smile in return.

"Plus, physical attraction and *caring* are two entirely different things."

His eyebrows pop. "Are you *finally* admitting to being attracted to me, Mercy?"

"No." I will never admit to that.

"Those girls don't do it for me anymore." His gaze drops downward, settling on the V-neckline of my sundress. "You, on the other hand, make me so hard I can't think straight when you're around."

Christ.

When those eyes flip up to meet mine, they're no longer a stormy blue; they're on fire. And his voice has taken on a new level of huskiness. "How much longer are you going to lie to yourself? The idea of riding my dick turns you on, doesn't it?"

"I'm not the one lying to myself." It's practically a whisper.

He settles his hands on the railing, his arms caging me in as he leans in, his mouth an inch from my ear. "Are you telling me that, if I were to put my hand under this little dress of yours and slide my fingers into your panties, that pretty pussy of yours wouldn't be as wet as it was yesterday when you undressed for me?"

My thighs quiver at the level of brash honesty and dirty talk coming from this man. The reality is, he has seen me completely naked and exposed already, and right now, despite how much I abhor him, he's right; I can feel the evidence soaking into my cotton panties.

Please do it, Gabriel.

Those words form unbidden in my mind for the first time as my fingers itch to touch his stomach, to inch lower and find out exactly how hard he is. What would it be like to forget all that's wrong with Gabriel and satisfy this growing physical need for him?

Probably mind-blowing.

"I need to work on my assignment," I manage, my voice thick with a level of desperation for him that I hate. "It's due in class tomorrow, and if I don't finish it, I'll fail the class. The prof is an asshole."

From behind and below, Caleb starts moaning—quick, deep, "oh" sounds that carry into the night, followed by one long, throaty cry.

Not until they've silenced do I realize that Gabriel's breaths are coming hard and fast.

And so are mine.

"Now you can eat in peace," he whispers, his words a kiss against my neck as he pulls away and heads for his patio door.

"Where are you going?" I blurt out before I can stop myself. I don't care, I tell myself.

Also a lie. I'd care if he was going down there with those women.

He pauses, gripping the door handle, his back to me. "To Empire for a few hours so you can get your assignment finished. I know school is important to you."

"Oh."

He peers over his shoulder at me. "Do me a favor and lock the bedroom door behind me when you go to bed."

"Why?" Panic spikes in my chest as the memory of Fleet's vicious eyes and determined hands hits me. "Is one of those guys going to try something on me?"

"No. You're safe. They would never touch you." His jaw tenses. "I would *kill* them if they tried."

A shiver runs down my spine. That's just an expression, right?

"Just ..." He hesitates, as if not wanting to admit something. "Women have a tendency of finding their way to my bedroom to wait for me to come home. And they're usually naked."

"Why am I not surprised," I mutter.

"If it's any consolation, there's only one naked woman I want to come home to tonight." He offers a lazy shrug and then a wry smile. "Just lock the door. Don't worry, I have a key." With that, he leaves.

I huff a sigh. Yeah, *that's* what I was worried about.

———

It's almost ten by the time I hit Save on my assignment. If I'd thought about it, I would have asked Gabriel about using the printer in his home office. I can't use the one at work, given this month's ink shortage, so I'll have to race across the city tomorrow to print it off at the campus library before class.

I shut my laptop and get ready for bed. The house has quieted for a bit; the constant thrum of music over the speakers ended around the time Gabriel left for the club—courtesy of him, I suspect. I assumed that Caleb and his "guests" had either left or were somewhere in the house, sleeping off the day of drinking and sunning and fucking.

But the music started up again an hour ago, followed by a rush of excited female screeches, as if more people had just arrived.

That's when I remembered to lock the bedroom door.

I can hear them outside now, their voices carrying from down below, and while the curious part of me wants to spy a little, another part knows I'll end up playing the "which ones has Gabriel fucked" game. I'm better off going to bed.

Normally the drive in to work is ten minutes, but being all the way out here, the commute to the other side of the city will be more like half an hour. Maybe more, depending on rush hour traffic. That means an early wake-up, which means I need to go to bed now, before Gabriel comes home and I have to face another round of his shamelessness. Just the thought stirs that unwelcome throb in me.

"Screw this." I sigh, cracking the cap on the Ambien, popping a pill, and setting my alarm.

22 GABRIEL

"Go ahead and make yourself comfortable," I mock, shoving Mike's size thirteens off my desk as I stroll by.

Our club manager gives me a wide grin in return, highlighting the gap between his front teeth. "Thought you weren't coming in tonight, boss."

"So did I." I pour myself a Hennessy. We don't open the doors for another hour, but staff is busy getting ready, stocking the bar, testing the sound system.

He sighs and clicks a few buttons, and the printer spits out an updated staff schedule. "What's your brother up to tonight?"

"Fucking, or about to fuck. Take your pick." I can tell when Caleb's trying to reduce his stress level through ejaculation. All this shit with our dad? It's causing major stress. Which means Caleb has dialed up at least five fresh, more-than-willing ladies for tonight.

That earns a deep laugh. "I swear, if I went at it like you two do, my heart would have given out by now."

189

"But what a way to go." I hold up my glass in salute before downing it, the burn down my throat welcome.

Mike is a beast of a man who casts shadows on all but two of our security team. He used to run a successful club on the Vegas strip that Caleb and I still frequent today when we head there. When we decided to open Empire, we knew we needed the best running this place, and the best was him. So we wined and dined him and offered him a shit ton of money to relocate. I swear, Caleb was ready to offer to suck his cock, he wanted him so bad.

And in hindsight, I would have let him because Mike is one of the reasons Empire is doing so well. He runs all the day-to-day. He's a smart guy. Coming from Vegas, he knows when to speak up about the business and when to shut his mouth and not ask questions.

He never asks why only Caleb and I run the final sales tallies.

Why we count the cash.

Why he's not involved in anything that has to do with the books.

"Speaking of going, are you two trying to kill me?"

I frown. "With what?"

"Caleb mentioned something about expanding to Vegas the other day." Mike's heavy dark brow furrows. "Was he talkin' out his ass or is that something you two are really considering?"

I chuckle. "Caleb's always talking out of his ass. But, yeah, it's an idea. We want to expand." Make a name for ourselves that has nothing to do with that damn drug trade or our father. Something that feels more urgent to me today than it did yesterday. "Why, you interested?" Frankly, we can't do it without his help.

Mike eases his mammoth body back into the office chair. It creaks in protest. "I've always said that I belong in Vegas."

———

I SHUT off the feed to the camera outside my bedroom. It looks like Mercy has gone to bed, the dim cast of light from the bedside lamp extinguished. A part of me can't wait to get home and slide into bed next to her.

But another part is beginning to dread it as this unexpected guilt creeps in. Will she ever be able to get past my family history? I've admitted to nothing, but that doesn't seem to matter to her. She's already guessed it, and correctly.

Yeah, she's attracted to me, and yeah, I'm helping her father for her. But am I just one step up from that fuckhead, Fleet, in her eyes?

I'm beginning to think so. She's been through a lot. Maybe I need to let her go. Consider her debt to me paid and leave her be. And if she decides she wants to give me a chance? She knows where to find me. That would be the considerate, selfless, gentlemanly thing to do.

If I could figure out how to be any of those things, maybe I could do it.

Mike pokes his head into the office. "There's two guys here, asking to come up and talk to you."

"Who?"

"They said their last name is Perri. They're waiting by the stairs."

A soft "fuck" slips out as I flip through Empire's camera feed, quickly locating the men in question. Merrick and Vince Perri, the youngest of the four Perri boys. Camillo Perri's children. What the hell are they doing, showing up here? Did my father get word to them? Did he send them here?

I sigh. "Send them up." This is going to be a fun game of I-don't-know-what-you- gentlemen-are-talking-about-we-know-nothing-about-that-drug-business-you-speak-of. Seriously, why the hell did the youngest Perri boys come all the way from San Diego to here? "Hey, Mike?" I call out before the door shuts completely. I level him with a look. "Search them, and station someone outside the door."

His deep brown eyes blink once, and he nods in understanding.

I check the hidden Glock on the underside of the desk, making sure it's loaded and the safety is off. And then I turn on the private security camera we have in here—that only Caleb and I are aware of and have access to—and wait.

Three minutes later, Vince and Merrick stroll in, their matching crystal-blue eyes roaming the interior of my office. We were all just teenagers the last time I last saw either of them in person. They've changed a lot—filled out and aged—but I guess so have I.

"Gabe, good to see you," Vince offers, his hands tucked casually into his pockets as he surveys the crowd down below through our one-way window. "We keep hearing great things about this place. We thought we'd check it out." He has a beard now. It's an improvement toward his masculinity, offsetting his girly long lashes and soft eyes.

"You didn't come here to check out the club. What do you two want?"

"Who says we want anything?" Merrick, six months younger than me and the youngest in the Perri family, asks. He takes after his mother more, with his dark blond hair and slender frame. Still, he's also bulked up with muscle compared to his gangly teenage version.

"Let me save you the trouble. Whatever my father may have told you, Caleb and I aren't interested in an alliance."

They exchange a glance. "Neither are we."

———

It's after two by the time I get home. The music and lights are all on, but no one's around. Only two cars sit in the driveway—aside from Mercy's hunk of shit. My guess is the owners of those cars are in Caleb's room with him.

Now's not the time to relay my conversation with the Perri boys. I'll wait until tomorrow, when he's sober.

Right now, I need to see Mercy.

I quietly unlock my bedroom door and enter. My nose catches her delicious floral scent immediately, and my blood stirs. I love that scent, whatever it is. Perfume? Shampoo? Skin cream? I don't know, but I love having my bedroom smell like her.

I want to smell like her.

I tiptoe around the bed to hit the switch that will lower the blackout blinds. I can't help but pause a moment to study her sleeping form in the moonlight. She's on her back, her long black hair fanning out over her pillow, her arms out on either side of her, her lips parted as slow, even breaths escape. The sheet is bunched around her waist, giving me a sublime view of her perky tits, her pebbled nipples poking the flimsy white cotton tank top.

She's the most beautiful woman I've ever laid eyes on. Part of me is beginning to regret not fucking her when she offered herself to me yesterday. But I'm no idiot; she didn't do that freely.

No … when she *really* wants it, when I see the unguarded lust in her eyes, that's when I'll give her the night of her life. My dick stirs with the thought, just as a pill bottle on her nightstand catches my eye. Careful not to rattle the pills, I lift the bottle, shining my phone on the label. Huh. Her father may refuse medication, but she doesn't. Then again, I guess I can't blame her with what she's been through lately.

Has she been on these long? The prescription fill date is two months ago. I crack the lid. It looks pretty full, which makes me think she filled the prescription in desperation but hasn't been taking them. They're a last resort, when she won't sleep otherwise.

Like a night lying in bed with me, because she couldn't drink herself to unconsciousness.

That same twinge of guilt that got me earlier stirs

now. The woman has been through hell, and while I may be helping her, I'm also making things worse.

I need to let her go.

Maybe tomorrow.

I gently set the bottle down, wondering if I need to be on alert. People do fucked-up shit on Ambien. Caleb was taking them a while back to help him sleep, until the night I caught him climbing into his Porsche, buck-naked, telling me we needed milk.

Caleb is lactose intolerant.

I reach out to drag the tip of my finger softly across her cheek. She doesn't stir, doesn't make a single sound. I doubt she'll be waking up until her alarm goes off. Which is set for … I open the alarm app on her phone. And groan. Five hours from now.

"Can't wait," I mutter, heading for the bathroom.

Ten minutes later, after I've showered the day off me and jerked my pent-up Mercy frustrations out, I'm ready to climb into bed and try to get some sleep.

I've barely touched the covers when Mercy lets out a moan. A soft, low moan that radiates need.

I freeze. She didn't make those sounds last night, but she was in an alcohol-induced coma. Does she normally moan like that in her sleep? Because if she does, I am *so* screwed—

"Gabriel …" It's a mere whisper, an erotic cry on her sleepy, plump lips.

"Fuck me," I hiss as blood rushes to my cock.

23 MERCY

THE MOON IS STILL high in the sky when I wake in Gabriel's bed.

The patio door is wide open.

Did I leave it open? I remember locking the bedroom door. I glance beside me to find the other side of the bed empty. A twinge of nervousness stirs as I climb out of bed and move to close it.

A tall male form fills a lounge chair on the patio. He's facing out over the valley but I know instantly that it's Gabriel, his delicious spicy scent caressing my senses ever so lightly.

Gabriel's home. Unexpected excitement stirs in my lower belly.

He's home, and his bare legs are splayed to settle on either side of the lounger. His arm is bent and moving up and down … up and down … up and down … in a smooth rhythm, the sound of skin rubbing against skin carrying into the quiet night air, along with his shallow, quick breaths.

I stifle my gasp.

Gabriel is stroking himself. It's an understanding that instantly sparks a painful throb between my legs. What does that beautiful man look like when he orgasms?

I *need* to know. It's a silent admission that doesn't come with the usual guilt or bitterness attached.

"Gabriel?" I call out, not wanting to startle him as I approach.

His arm freezes for two … three … four beats before it starts up again, this time a touch slower, as if he's trying to draw the act out.

I round the chair to take in the full view of a magnificently naked Gabriel, his fist wrapped tightly around that big, perfect cock of his, sliding from root to tip over and over again. The pink head reaches nearly to his belly button. A bead of cum leaking from it glows in the bright moonlight.

It's the most mouthwatering sight I've ever taken in.

"This is for you." His head is resting against the back of the chair, tipped back to expose his thick neck and that sexy jagged bump in the center of his throat that I desperately want to lick. It's not all I want to lick. I drag my gaze down the expanse of his impressive chest, over his round, pebbled nipples, his chiseled six-pack, that appealing vee of his hips …

By the time my eyes settle on his dick again, I'm practically panting, my body humming with need.

And I can't resist him anymore.

I feel like I'm on autopilot, reaching for my pajama shorts, hooking my thumbs beneath the elastic band, pushing them and my panties down until they fall onto the concrete.

Gabriel's eyes ignite with fire. He reaches out with his free hand. "Come here, baby."

I love it when he calls me that, I decide, slipping my fingers through his, reveling in the feel of his callouses against my palm as he pulls me toward him. I part my legs to straddle the width of the chair—and him—and edge my way forward until I'm standing over his hips.

"Do you want me?" He stops stroking himself and holds his impressive cock upward.

"Yes," I admit, and the moment the word escapes my lips, a weight lifts off my chest. "Yes, Gabriel. I want you." Despite everything, despite knowing he's all wrong, I want him.

Releasing my hand, he slides his fingers up my inner thigh, all the way to the apex. He drags his index finger back and forth along my slit. My knees quake under his teasing touch. "You're dripping," he murmurs, and then he's pushing that finger deep into me.

My sex flexes around it.

"Jesus. So, so wet. And so tight." He begins pumping in and out of me, first with that one finger, then with a second, all while his thumb draws languid circles over my clit. "I can't wait to fill you."

"What *are* you waiting for?" My body begins to tremble as I roll my hips against his hand, allowing him to finger fuck me, ever aware of how exposed I am out here. The security cameras … they're catching all of this.

I don't care.

He pulls his hand away, seizing the backs of my knees, the fingers from his one hand slick against my skin. "I need you. *Please.* Mercy. Let me have you tonight." There's an air of desperation in his tone as he gently tugs at my legs, trying to get me to buckle.

I feel the seductive smile spread across my lips. "Are you begging me, Gabriel?"

"I'll get on my knees if you want," he whispers hoarsely.

God, I want this.

I want Gabriel.

I reach down to grasp him—his skin is hot and velvety smooth—and line his thick head up with my opening.

My body stretches wide as Gabriel sinks deep inside me, the feeling both erotic and overwhelming, eliciting a deep cry from my—

I feel rather than hear the cry that escapes my throat as I wake in Gabriel's bed, my breathing ragged, my body trembling. My hand down the front of my shorts, my fingers buried inside myself.

Oh my God, that was only a dream.

Disappointment hits me.

I'm so bewildered by the jarring end to what was shaping up to be the most stimulating dream of my life that it's a few seconds before I notice the dim light being cast from the other side of the bed.

And another second before I turn to discover Gabriel lying in bed next to me, propped up on one elbow, his lips parted, his breathing equally ragged.

A look of unguarded awe on his face.

He swallows hard. "Christ, baby. That was so fucking hot." It's a strangled growl, his hooded gaze darting between my face and where my hand still hides beneath the sheet, my legs splayed. I'm not the only one touching myself, I note. The sheet sits dangerously low on his sculpted abdomen and does nothing to disguise that his fist is wrapped around his swollen dick.

"You were dreaming about me," he says huskily, and it's not a question. There's also not a hint of his usual arrogance.

"It felt so real," I admit, sounding a bit stunned. So vivid. Embarrassment that Gabriel was watching me touch myself hasn't yet set in. Is *this* real? Or am I still dreaming? I do feel a bit discombobulated, but that could be because all my blood is being channeled into this deep throb between my legs, an aching need to follow through with this release. "You begged me." *And I wanted it.*

I still want it.

Hunger flashes in his molten eyes as he studies my face a moment. "Is that what you need?" He slides his hand out from under the sheets and gently pushes a strand of hair off my forehead in an unexpectedly affectionate way, before dragging his thumb across my bottom lip. "You want me to beg you?"

Honestly? I don't think I care at this moment.

What I really want is to feel what I felt in that dream.

He eases the sheet down off us, and I lose my breath at his naked body. It's as perfect as the version in my dream. I slip my hand from my shorts.

"No," he commands softly, collecting it within his and bringing it to his lips.

I let out a tiny sound as he slides the two fingers that were inside me into his mouth, sucking on them a moment, a low, appreciative moan in his throat as he releases them. He guides my hand back to my shorts, his fingers overlapping mine as he pushes down past the elastic to settle between my legs. His fingers work my wet ones over my clit like a master puppeteer.

My head sinks back into my pillow with a gasp. A few minutes of this and I'm going to be riding our fingers to ecstasy in front of him, and for whatever reason, I need that right now.

He shifts closer until his naked body is pressed against my side. His skin is burning hot, but I welcome it. He dips his head down into the crook of my neck and places a lingering sweet kiss against my throat. His mouth finds my ear. "Mercy ..." My body shudders with the depth of his voice in my ear. "Please let me fuck you tonight. I'm begging."

"Yes. Okay," I murmur. What is this spell I've fallen under? This heady, intoxicating dream that I don't want to wake from. This low buzz that courses through my veins.

Whatever it is, I'm going with it.

I reach up with my free hand to weave my fingers through his silky hair. It's the perfect length to fist. I do that now, pulling his head back. Our eyes meet. "Kiss me?"

He hesitates but only for a second, and then his mouth is eagerly sealing over mine, his plush lips working like he suddenly can't get enough, his tongue sliding across the seam of my lips, prying my mouth open, diving in to swirl and tease and explore my mouth.

"I like kissing you," I admit between pants.

"Not as much as you're going to like fucking me," he promises, pushing two of his fingers deep inside my opening. "Shit," he chokes. "You're so tight."

"I know." I nip at his bottom lip with my teeth.

A deep sound rattles in his chest, and then it's as if he's been unleashed. Yanking his hand out of my shorts, he reaches between my legs and, feeding his fingers and thumb through the leg holes to fist the material, he tugs my shorts and panties down off. "Lift your legs up," he demands, and I comply, making it easy for him to slip them off my ankles.

He wastes no time, shifting to kneel between my legs, his strong, rough hands pushing my thighs out, spreading me wide for him. My body is on fire despite the cool air, my mind swirling in an intoxicating cloud, desperate to have those dark eyes touch every inch of me.

I ease the hem of my tank top up over my waist, over my breasts, over my head, tossing it somewhere into the corner.

"I could stare at your naked body all day long." He gives his straining cock a lazy stroke, rolling his thumb over the tip, and it's so much like my dream. A tingling sensation begins to build along my spine as I memorize this image of him.

"I'm going to come if you keep doing that." I stretch

my legs wider and rock my hips, inviting him in as a rush of heat flows to my pelvis.

"Yeah, you will. On my tongue, first," he growls, diving down to fit his broad shoulders between my thighs, his strong hands seizing either side and pushing them so far apart, my muscles strain.

I gasp, my body tensing as the tip of his tongue swirls before flattening and ever so slowly dragging through my center.

He pauses to flash a cocky grin and throw a wink, and then his mouth closes over my slit, and he gets to work, licking and sucking like a starving man being nourished, breaking frequently to tongue-fuck me, his fingers parting my folds. His moan of pleasure each time vibrates through my core.

My eyes roll back in my head.

This is almost too intense; Gabriel's passion, his skill … almost too much to bear. I come in minutes with my hands gripping his hair tightly and my hips bucking against his beautiful face, riding a seemingly endless current of orgasm as I cry out, until I'm nothing but quivering, boneless mess, my body sinking into the mattress, deeper and deeper and …

24 GABRIEL

"Mercy?"

Her eyes are closed, her body unmoving, her long, slender legs splayed, showcasing that sweet-tasting pussy that I just ravaged with my mouth, that I'm thinking I could eat out morning, noon, and night every day for the rest of my life and never be sick of.

"Mercy," I call again, warily this time, shifting to loom over her.

Her breathing is slow and shallow.

"You've gotta be fucking kidding me," I mutter, astonished. Minutes ago she was humping my face and screaming my name. Now she's dead-to-the-world asleep?

My gaze darts to the nightstand. Shit. This has to be the Ambien. It must have sparked whatever wild, erotic dream she had before waking up.

If she was even awake.

Fuck.

I fall back into bed with a groan. My body is a live

wire, the ache in my balls painful, my cock throbbing. I was seconds away from blowing all over the sheets when Mercy came. Somehow I resisted the urge, the promise of shoving my dick inside her too good to pass up.

She seemed lucid though, didn't she? Wild-eyed, maybe. Definitely pulled a one-eighty in the "please fuck me" department as compared to her usual frostiness. But there was nothing about her that hinted she may be on an Ambien high and unaware of what was going on.

Will she remember coming on my face? I sure as hell know I won't forget it. I drag my tongue across my bottom lip, catching the sweet taste of her all over my mouth.

Or is she going to wake up and wonder why she's naked? Wonder what *I did* to her? Screw that. I ain't about *that* life.

But I begged her. I've never begged a woman to fuck me before. I've barely ever even had to ask. It's always more a casual mention. Better yet, I just have to unfasten my belt. And yet I would have gotten on my knees and pleaded with this woman to let me inside her.

And she fucking fell asleep on me.

I gently tug at the sheet caught beneath her and drawing it over her perfect, sleeping form. I guess we'll see what she remembers in a few hours, when her alarm goes off.

For now … I look down at my swollen dick. "Yeah, I know, buddy." I give it a slow stroke, my thumb spreading out the stickiness pooling at the top. I was really hoping to see Mercy's lips around it at some point tonight, to feel the softness of her hair in my grip and the back of her throat as she sucked on it.

Maybe tomorrow.

Or maybe I'll wake up to her murdering me.

With a sigh, I climb out of bed and head for another hot shower. I haven't jerked off like this since I was thirteen years old.

What is this woman doing to me?

25 MERCY

I PAW for my phone to check the time. 5:40 a.m. I can get another twenty minutes of sleep before my alarm goes off and I have to get—

I'm naked.

My groggy eyes widen with shock as fuzzy pieces begin to click.

Gabriel, out on the patio.

Gabriel, in this bed.

Gabriel's face, between my legs.

I stifle the gasp that threatens to escape.

Did I ask Gabriel to fuck me last night?

Did he beg me to let him fuck me?

Did we fuck out on the patio?

Ever so slowly, I roll onto my back. Gabriel's on his stomach, his muscular arms folded over his pillow, his breathing slow and steady. He's still asleep, thank God. His face is peaceful. Almost boyish, despite the shadow of stubble forming, his lashes a long, dark fringe around his eyes, his lips plump and red, parted ever so slightly.

The bedsheet slipped down his back—his glorious, rippled back—during the night and now it sits low on his hips, just above the swell of his hard, round ass.

Oh my God. This is like waking up after a night of drunken debauchery, wondering what happened. Except, I vividly remember certain parts. I'm just not sure how much of it is real?

I'm naked, so something definitely happened.

I spy my tank top over by the patio door, where I vaguely remember tossing it. That part must have been real. Okay. So … Gabriel's face was likely between my legs last night, his skilled mouth bringing me to an orgasm of godly proportions. A deep ache ignites between my legs with the memory of his light stubble scraping against my skin, of his tongue lapping, pushing into me, his lips sucking on me.

But I remember nothing after that.

Before that … I fucked Gabriel on the patio, but then woke up in bed next to him. I thought that was the dream, but maybe it was a dream within a dream—a sex inception. Or maybe all of this was real. Or maybe none of it was a dream … All I remember is that I wanted Gabriel with every fiber of my being last night, in real life or imaginary. It was as if every instinct I've ever had about the guy vanished, every safeguard was tripped.

But I also remember him being considerate. Passionate. Not an arrogant, crass jerk; not an egomaniac. He called me baby like he meant it; he looked at me with excitement and, dare I say, admiration?

He seemed genuinely interested in pleasing me.

He begged me.

This is all the fault of that stupid pill I took. I'm going to find out which pharmaceutical company manufactures them and I'm going to write them a letter demanding they warn patients of the risk of *extremely* erotic dreams that make you do insane, reckless things like let hot but dangerous men go down on you.

I am never, *ever* taking Ambien again, I silently vow, my mind and stomach swirling with a mix of emotion I can't begin to grasp. All I know is that I can't face Gabriel right now. I have to get the hell out of here before he wakes up.

Shutting off my alarm, I slip out of bed and tiptoe my naked ass toward the bathroom, grabbing the work clothes I set out on the dresser.

Five minutes later, after a hasty washing up—I skipped the shower, afraid the sound might stir Gabriel —I'm sneaking through the house, intent on getting to the front door. A bout of coughing warns me that someone is awake and in the kitchen before I pass through.

It doesn't warn me that said someone—Caleb—is naked.

"Jesus!" I turn away but not before getting a good full-frontal glimpse of Gabriel's brother as he chugs orange juice straight from the carton, his dick hanging low and flaccid.

"Sorry. Didn't expect anyone up." He lets out a deep belch. He doesn't sound the least bit sorry. He looks rough—his jaw covered in two-day stubble, his brown hair standing on end, his eyes bleary and red—like he's coming off a day of drinking heavily and a night of fucking frequently. *Oh, wait ...*

"Do you mind if I make myself a coffee?" I'm going to need it to deal with traffic. Then again, I'm leaving so early, maybe I'll avoid the worst of it.

"Have at it. Machine's there. Mugs are above it." He waves a hand toward the corner. "You want me to run it for you?"

Gabriel's naked brother making me coffee ... while naked? "I think I'll manage. Thanks." I set my school bag and purse down, doing my best to avoid Caleb. The kitchen is a mess. Dirty dishes, leftover food, pizza boxes, spilled drinks. Their poor housekeeper is going to have her hands full.

"What are you doing up anyway?"

"I'm going to work."

"Work?" He says it like it's a foreign word.

"You know, that thing people living in the real world do. Get up early, drag themselves into an office to earn a paycheck?"

He chuckles, turning to slide the carton back into the fridge. I steal a glance. Yeah, his ass is almost as nice as Gabriel's. "What are you saying? That Gabe and me don't live in the real world?" He turns back faster than I expect, catching my gaze on him.

"Can you *please* cover up?" I ask, my cheeks burning.

With a heavy sigh, he reaches for a red hand towel by the sink and holds it up over his front with one hand. "How's this?"

"It'll do. Thanks." *Note to self: don't use the red hand towel.* I find a travel mug in the cupboard—perfect.

Popping the coffee pod in, I set it to brew. For all the fancy toys and wealth these two have, I'm happy to see a normal coffee maker that us mere mortals can operate.

"You hungry?"

"No."

"You sure? Rosita stuffed the fridge. There's …" He opens the heavy metal door again and peruses the contents. "Grapes … apples … strawberries … yogurt. Shit, I haven't had yogurt in forever. Oh, lemon-flavored. She knows that one's my favorite."

I shake my head. "You sound like a teenage boy raiding the kitchen after his mom has come home from a Saturday shop."

"Yeah, I wouldn't know what that was like."

I catch a distinct shift in his light, unbothered tone. A sharp edge that slips in. What button did I just push?

"Thanks though," I offer after a moment. "I'm not a big morning eater. I'll just grab something near work."

"Where do you work?"

"Mary's Way. It's a drug addiction center."

"A drug addiction …" His voice drifts as he takes that information in. And then his head falls back and he bursts out with laughter. "Oh Gabe, you sure do pick 'em," he says to the ceiling.

"What is that supposed to mean?" I ask.

He levels me with a knowing look, but doesn't elaborate. He doesn't have to. We both know where their vast amounts of money come from, though neither he nor Gabriel will ever admit to it.

"Do you have cream?" I ask as the machine finishes brewing.

He answers with a childish giggle.

I shake my head. "What is it with you two and that stupid joke?"

"Ah, so you've heard that one already." He saunters over to set the carton on the counter beside me. "This is all the cream I can manage for you right now, babe. I think the girls broke my dick last night."

"Thanks." Girls. Plural.

He pauses there, and I'm ever aware of his looming presence, his giant, muscular body, and his nakedness. "From what I heard last night, it sounded like you might have broken my brother's dick, too."

"No, we didn't …" I manage to stutter, my face bursting into flames. Oh my God. It *did* happen.

"Well, someone sure made you happy. I came down here to grab a drink and, damn, were you ever screaming."

I slap the lid onto my cup and edge around him, grabbing my bags on my way toward the front door.

"Hold up." Caleb laughs. "Seriously, wait up. You'll set off the alarm."

I linger by the door, huddled in my arms, desperate to get away before Gabriel wakes and I have to deal with him teasing me, too.

Caleb takes his time strolling over. At least he's still covering himself with the hand towel. His fingers move fast over the keypad, followed by a thumbprint scan. "There. You're a free bird now. Fly away." He opens the door, holding it for me. "Have a good day, honey."

I beeline for my car, praying it'll start.

"Oh, hey, Mercy?" Caleb calls.

Like an idiot, I instantly turn back.

"In case you were wondering"—he drops his hand and the towel that covers his growing erection —"Gabriel is willing to share."

"Noted." I rush for my car, desperate to get away from this hell house.

26 GABRIEL

Mercy's side of the bed is empty when I wake. With a sluggish roll, I reach for my phone. 9:07 a.m. I must have slept through her alarm.

I groan into my pillow. Shit. I wanted to talk to her before she left, to figure out where her head is at. See if she remembers what happened or if she woke up naked and freaked out and assumed I did something unwelcome to her.

Despite this sordid arrangement we've got going on, I told her I wouldn't hurt her and I meant it.

But does she believe me?

I reach for my phone, intent on calling her and clearing things up.

"Yo!" A fist thumps once on the door and then Caleb is strolling into my room. "Rosita's here and she is *pissed* at us," he says around a mouthful of cornflakes, spilling milk over his bare chest in the process. At least he's put on some sweatpants. Rosita's the only one he'll go out of his way to do that for.

"What'd she say?" I croak, my throat still thick with sleep.

"Dunno. It was all in Spanish but I definitely heard her call you a *puta*."

I burst out laughing. "As if." Rosita is the sweetest lady I've ever met. Our mom hired her when I was just seven. Why she keeps putting up with our sorry asses all these years later, I can't fathom. Probably because we pay her better than anyone else would. It also might have to do with her knowing who our father is and not wanting to upset us by leaving.

"Come on. Get dressed." He kicks the end of my bed. "Eighteen holes. Let's go."

"Are you nuts? It's way too hot for that shit." January, February … hell, even May, I'd be in. But midday golfing in July in the desert?

Fuck that shit.

"I helped your captive escape earlier."

I frown at the sudden change of topic. "What?"

"Mercy. She ducked out around six this morning. I lifted the alarm so she could get out."

The alarm. I hadn't thought of that. But wait. "So you saw her this morning? You talked to her?"

"Uh-huh." He chews while still somehow managing a shit-eating grin.

Which means it was a proud hang-out-with-your-wang-out moment for him.

"How was she? Did she seem rattled? Upset?"

"Nah. Tired. Annoyed. She didn't seem to like being teased about all the screaming you had her doing last night. Bravo, little brother. For a woman who wanted to choke the life out of you only days ago ..." He shakes his head and chuckles.

I pinch the bridge of my nose. "Did she seem like she remembered it?"

"Oh, she remembered. Her face turned red fast, man." He laughs again, but then frowns. "Wait, why wouldn't she remember? Did she get into my vodka again?"

"No." I sigh and nod toward her nightstand. "Remember what happened when *you* took Ambien?"

"Yeah. *Oh* ..." Realization sinks in. "So you think that's why she was willing to let you bone her?"

I rub my forehead. "Who knows." I sure as hell don't. It's not like I know the woman. I'm just forcing her to stay in my house, sleep in my bed. Normal stuff.

He snickers to himself as he scoops a few mouthfuls of soggy cereal into his mouth.

"Well ... if I know women at all—and I do"—he smirks—"she definitely remembered what went on. I just can't tell you what she thinks about it."

I fall back in my pillow and stare up at the ceiling.

"And seriously, bro, you had to pick the one that works at an *addiction* center."

I groan. "I know."

"What do you think she's gonna do when she finds out who we are? Fall head over heels madly in love with you?"

"Okay, first of all, who the fuck is talking about love here? Have you been binging on those Hallmark movies again?" I rub my brow. Sometimes my brother is too much. "And she already looked up Dad and thinks we're into it."

"No wonder she hates you."

"Yeah, no shit." Maybe more now than before.

Caleb snaps his fingers. "Oh, anything exciting happen at Empire last night?"

I release a second groan. "If you call Vince and Merrick Perri paying us a visit exciting."

Caleb's metal spoon clatters in his bowl, his face hardening. "You're kidding me, right?"

"I wish."

"They had the fucking nerve to show up at Empire? What for?"

"They want an alliance—"

"That son of a bitch reached out to them from inside? There's no fucking way we're doing this!" Caleb's temper flares, his eyes brimming with rage.

"No. You don't get it. Not an alliance against the cartel." The two youngest Perris are more like Caleb and me than I'd like to admit: they're looking for a way out of the drug business too. I level my brother with a look. "They want an alliance against our fathers."

27 MERCY

MARSHA POPS her head into my little corner cubicle just as I'm finishing up court documentation for Polly Hudgins, a drug addict who lost custody of her children and has checked in to Mary's diligently every day for the past two months, sober, in her attempt to get them back. "Did Darlene O'Neill come through here?"

"No. Was she supposed to?"

Marsha frowns. When she frowns, she look downright sinister. "She was waiting out in the lobby and now she's gone. And no one's seen her."

"Maybe she just ducked out to grab lunch?" It is almost noon.

"Hmm ..." She's not convinced. "She seemed on edge."

"Give her a chance to come back," I suggest, but even I'm not buying that excuse. Spend enough time around drug addicts and you get really good at reading the signs—twitchiness, jumpy, anxious, in a rush. Chances are Darlene O'Neill fell off the wagon last night, did the right thing by coming in today, but needed a fix too bad to stay.

Marsha makes to leave, but then pauses. "You okay? You look tired."

"I'm exhausted, actually," I admit. For reasons she'd *never* suspect.

Worry fills her round face. "How's your dad doing?"

"As well as can be." I sigh. "He was hospitalized last week for a punctured lung."

By the time I'm done recounting the details, Marsha's mouth is hanging wide, her hand pressed against her ample chest. "You need to talk to the guards. Or the warden."

"I tried, but it doesn't sound like I'm going to get anywhere with that. Prison rules and all that."

Her lips twist. "I'll pray for him. And you, that you get to see him soon."

I avert my gaze to my computer screen. "Thank you. I appreciate it." I feel like I'm lying to her—I've already seen him—but Marsha would never understand the arrangement I've fallen into with Gabriel. Hell, *I* don't understand it. Even less, now.

Her demeanor shifts suddenly to one radiating energy. "You know what, girl? You work so hard. Why don't you take an extra thirty for your lunch break today? On me. Get out, stretch your legs a bit, eat. The sun and warmth will do you some good."

"Maybe I will. Thanks." I haven't had anything but a coffee today.

"You do that. I don't want to see you back here until

one fifteen. That's an order." With a pat against my cubicle wall, she strolls off, humming to herself.

My phone vibrates against my desk, and my heart stutters at the now-familiar number that pops up. Gabriel's texting me. *Again.* The fact that I never gave him my number is not lost on me.

Gabriel: Stop ignoring me. It's annoying and childish.

He's annoyed. Right. I scroll through the four other text messages he already sent me this morning.

Gabriel: Call me when you get this.

Gabriel: We need to talk about last night.

Gabriel: When's your lunch break?

Gabriel: Nothing happened … beyond what you remember.

This last text is of a less friendly tone than the others.

And what does he mean about nothing happening beyond what I remember? Did he figure out I was not of sound mind, and if so, when exactly did he come to that conclusion? *While* his tongue was between my legs or *after*? My body stirs with excitement at that memory, but I tamp it down. How does he even know what I remember about last night?

His brother. Caleb must have told him about our early morning conversation.

I study the sequence of messages again. If I didn't know better, I'd say Gabriel sounds worried. Or guilty.

The red light on my desk phone begins flashing with a call from the reception desk.

"Hey, Ali, what's up?"

"*Hey*, Mercy," our bubbly receptionist drawls, and I can just picture her twirling her long blond strands in her fingertips. "So, there's a guy here to see you. He said his name is Gabriel. You know him, right?"

My stomach explodes in flutters. Oh my God. "Yes. I know him." Gabriel came to my place of work?

"Did you want to come out?" I hear the real question in Ali's wary voice: Do we need to call the police? After what happened with Fleet, everyone's a bit more cautious about guys showing up at Mary's looking for me.

I don't want to come out, but something tells me Gabriel won't take kindly to that answer. I guess I'll have to face him—and last night's dirty escapade—now.

"Yeah, I'll be there in a sec. Tell him to wait for me outside." We're a facility for women, and many of those women are or were in abusive relationships with men. As a general rule, Marsha does not let men loiter around.

Dropping the receiver onto the base with a groan, I make sure my desk is locked—anything worth pawning for cash to buy drugs is too tempting around this place —grab my purse, and head for the door, steeling my nerve to face him.

At least he did as asked and went outside, I note, because I don't see him at reception.

Ali's eyes are as round of saucers when they meet mine. "Okay, *who* is *that?*" She enunciates each word

"Just someone I know. A friend," I lie.

"A friend? *Please* tell me you're sleeping with your friend."

My cheeks flush. "No."

"But you want to—"

"No."

"But you've thought about it—"

"See you after lunch." I slide my sunglasses on—armor against Gabriel's penetrating gaze—and, taking a deep breath, I step out into the hot desert sun.

The sight of Gabriel steals that breath from my lungs in a heartbeat. He's perched on the back of a jet-black SUV, his jeans-clad legs splayed, his arms folded over his broad torso, his gaze seemingly on Mary's Place, though I can't tell behind the shiny aviator glasses covering his eyes.

He's styled his hair differently today, too, his brown locks swept back lazily as if with his hand. It's a casual look but downright sexy.

And he didn't shave.

I clear my throat as I approach him, my steps measured. The heat is a welcome change from the chilly air inside, especially against my bare legs. "You can't just show up here like this."

"Why not?"

"Because people will start asking me who you are. The receptionist just did."

I get a one-sided smirk in response. "What'd you tell her?"

God. I kissed those lips last night. Actually, I didn't *just* kiss them. I sucked on them. I licked them. I bit them.

I came on them.

I clear my throat. "That you're a pain in my ass."

That smirks morphs into a downright devilish smile, dimples and all. "Oh, baby, I *can* be. Though I'd make sure it isn't painful for you."

My mouth goes dry, and it takes a few swallows to find my tongue. "What do you want, Gabriel. I need to grab lunch and get back to work." If he's feeling guilty about last night, he's hiding it well.

"What exactly do you remember?" he asks suddenly, his voice shifting to something more serious.

"What *should* I remember?" I counter. Will Gabriel admit to the truth? I hesitate, glancing around us to make sure no one's listening. "Were we out on the patio at all last night?"

"No."

"So, that *was* a dream." Oddly enough, the wave of relief I'm expecting to feel with this confirmation doesn't come.

He slides his sunglasses off, revealing a serious gaze as he studies me. "When I came home, you were already asleep in bed. You cried out my name—"

"Okay, I don't need specifics—"

"And then you slid your hand down your shorts—"

"Gabriel!" I glare at him, blushing furiously.

He grins. "How long is your lunch break?"

I hesitate but decide on the truth versus a lie. "An hour and fifteen today. My boss said I needed the extra time." And Marsha's not kidding—if I step foot in this building before one fifteen, she'll kick me out.

"Perfect." He stands and heads for the passenger side of the SUV, opening the door. "Get in."

I don't move.

"Look, we need to talk," he says with a hint of annoyance. "We can either do it here in the parking lot or over lunch. Me? I'd rather go someplace else." He nods to the building behind me. "This place is a shithole."

I'm not concerned about his opinion of Mary's Way, but I don't want visitors or my coworkers overhearing anything that might come out of his filthy mouth. With a heavy sigh of reluctance, I march forward and climb in. The SUV may not be the Lamborghini but it's still posh with a capital "I'm worth more than you'll make in the next five years"—black leather, upgraded *everything*.

And it smells like Gabriel's deliciously spicy cologne, that scent that's been lingering in my nostrils since the moment I woke up. I try to hide my deep inhale as he climbs in and cranks the engine.

Last night has changed our dynamic, I realize with dismay. I can feel it. I was attracted to him before, while hating him. Now though? Now that I've actually felt his hot, naked flesh pressed against my body, his forearms hooked around my thighs, his stubble between my legs, his talented tongue *inside* me?

Now, despite still hating him, those things are all I can think about, especially as I watch his fingers smooth over the steering wheel. My arousal is growing in my lower belly.

"What do you feel like having?"

I grit my teeth against the bubble of hysterical laughter that threatens to burst.

You. I feel like having you, jackass.

I have to turn away, so he can't see my blush.

I can't believe it. I *want* Gabriel.

The bastard was right all along, and it only took two days.

———

"It looks kind of dumpy during the day." My gaze wanders down the back alley behind Empire to the Dumpster and the broken glass surrounding it. It's nothing more than a warehouse, a huge rectangle of gray steel.

"All clubs do." Gabriel unlocks the door and steps inside, disarming the beeping alarm in seconds.

Whereas the outside seems rather ordinary and industrial, the inside of the vast club is downright creepy. Eerie silence greets us as we move along the same passageway that Gabriel led me down the night I was here with Michelle, our hollow footfalls echoing through the emptiness.

He flips open a black panel on the wall and begins flicking switches, and suddenly there's light illuminating the black walls and polished concrete floors and lengthy bar.

"It's clean," I remark.

Gabriel chuckles. "What did you expect?"

"I don't know. Sticky floors, used condoms." I inhale the scent of ammonia. "Stale booze?"

"We'd end up with rats and roaches if we left it like that." He leads me to the far end of the club and up a set of steps. "A crew was in here at four this morning, cleaning everything." Setting our takeout containers of salad on one end of a long table in the VIP section, he gestures for me to sit. "Want a drink?"

I hold up my Coke in answer.

"Want something to *add* to that drink?" He nods toward the bar.

I raise an eyebrow. "So I can go back to my job at an *alcohol* and drug addiction center smelling of booze?"

He sighs. "Fine, come on. We've got forty minutes, so … eat." He gently herds me into the leather banquette with a warm hand against my lower back, his fingers splayed wide, his pinky stroking dangerously close to the crack of my ass. But, unlike when that drunken creep Lawrence pulled that same move on me a little over a week ago here, I don't seem to mind it now.

I release a shaky breath as I shimmy in. He slides in right after me, allowing for no room between us, though there is seating for at least ten people here, possibly more. We spend a quiet, tense minute opening cutlery and ripping apart dressing packets.

Gabriel clears his throat. "When I told you I would never force myself on you, I wasn't lying." His voice is oddly somber; there isn't the slightest hint of his usual obnoxiousness. He pokes at the chicken in his dish with his fork, but he doesn't collect any. "Last night, I was lying in bed next to you. I knew you were dreaming. About me. You said my name more than once. It was the fucking hottest thing I've ever watched." His eyes flash to mine and there's no mistaking the lust in them.

My heart races.

"Then you woke up all of a sudden, with this wild

sexed-up look, and I asked you if you wanted me. You said yes." He studies my mouth for a long moment. "You asked me to kiss you, so I did. And then I went down on you." His lips curl with a secretive smile. "And after you came——"

My breath hitches, remembering the tidal wave that ripped through me and the feel of Gabriel's expert mouth on me.

"You fell asleep. You were out cold." A rare softness touches his expression. "That's when I clued in. I saw the pills on your nightstand earlier and I know how messed-up people can get on them. Crazy dreams, hallucinations, that sort of thing."

"That would make sense." The last thing I remember is orgasming and then nothing. Because I was passed out.

Gabriel must have been horny as hell. I swallow. "So what'd you do then?"

He shrugs. "I covered you up, jerked off in the shower, and went to sleep. Prayed to God that you didn't wake up thinking I'd done something to you while you were unconscious."

My shoulders sink with relief, and it's quickly followed by a sympathetic warmth blooming in my chest. This explains all the phone calls and the impromptu arrival at my work. Gabriel Easton has a decent side after all. Maybe more decent than some of the guys I've dated in the past. Who knew? Definitely not me.

But his father is a damn crime boss! A murdering-and-money-laundering-and-witness-tampering-oh-my!

crime boss. Gabriel and his family have gotten rich off helping weak people pump their veins with drugs until they die. He doesn't feel guilty about anything, and I can't feel sympathy for him.

Beneath the table, Gabriel's warm hand settles on my knee and his thumb begins stroking my bare skin in an affectionate way. I don't feel the immediate urge to shoo his touch away. *Shit, shit, shit* … things are definitely —and quickly—changing between us, whether I want them to or not. "I thought you were awake, Mercy." His dark blue eyes are full of earnest. "If I'd had any idea you weren't, I wouldn't have—"

"I was awake," I find myself admitting out loud, drawing his gaze back to mine. "I mean, I guess I kind of wasn't because I was messed up, but I remember *everything*. Vividly."

Gabriel's thumb pauses. "Yeah?"

I bite my lip to squash the small smile that threatens, but in the end I let him see it. "Yeah."

I remember.

Every.

Erotic.

Second.

He lets out a heavy sigh of relief, and my heart stutters. I never would have expected this from him.

"Tell me you don't regret it."

I open my mouth—

"Don't lie to me, Mercy," he demands, his voice husky, a threatening storm in his gaze. "Please. Don't. Lie."

If I answer that truthfully, I'll be committing myself

to whatever indecent path Gabriel is intent on leading me down. But I don't know that I care anymore. My life is complicated and impossibly hard. For once I'd like something to be easy.

Sex with Gabriel—hot, dirty, immoral sex—would be easy. And, if last night is any indication … mind-blowing.

Oh shit. I take a deep breath. And then shake my head.

His thumb begins stroking my knee again, and there's a distinctive shift from a moment ago, the way it drags rather than draws, the intention in it skittering all the way up my inner thigh. It takes half a thought to resurrect the feeling of his fingers inside me again, a memory that makes me sigh longingly.

"Are you wet right now?"

"Yes." A resigned chuckle escapes me as I flop back into the banquette. "I can't believe I'm admitting that to you."

"I'm glad you are. *Finally.*"

I roll my eyes, but smile. "But I'm not one of your groupies. I won't beg you for anything, so I hope you've gotten that idea out of your thick skull."

Gabriel pushes our untouched lunches off to the side. He turns his big body toward me, leveling me with an intense gaze. "That's fine. I think I'd rather beg you." In the next second, his strong hands are around my waist and I'm being hoisted onto the table.

28 GABRIEL

I'VE FUCKED a lot of women.

I've fucked a lot of women in Empire—in the office, on the bar; yes, on these tables.

But I'll admit, as I stare up at the sexy woman perched in front of me, her legs parted, her body trembling with excitement, her dark brown eyes flaring with the unbridled lust I've been longing to see, there is no way I've ever wanted inside a woman this bad.

Just the anticipation of feeling the tip of my dick sink into her has my balls tightening.

I give the material of her dress a tug. "Take this off." It's a cute dress—blue with bright orange flowers splattered all over the bottom half. It'll be a cute, ripped, cum-stained dress in another minute if it doesn't disappear.

She glances over her shoulder. "Are you sure no one's going to come in?"

"No one's going to come in, baby." I'm not used to modesty from any of my women, and I'm finding that it only turns me on more. "But we don't have a lot of time before we have to leave, so unless you plan on telling your boss why you're late, you better get moving." My voice sounds too low and harsh to me, but by the way her body just shuddered now, I don't think she minds.

As she wiggles and shimmies and lifts her dress over her head, uncovering her lace underthings and that tight, beautiful body, I make quick work of my belt buckle and fly. Fishing my wallet—and condom—out of my back pocket, I push my jeans and boxers down to my hips.

I give my dick a slow stroke. I don't know if it's ever been this hard before. Oh yeah, it has … last night.

Neatly setting the dress off to the side, Mercy hesitates a moment and then reaches behind her. The straps of her lace bra slide down her arms and suddenly I'm staring at her perky breasts again, my mouth watering at how perfectly round and hard and pink her nipples are. I need all afternoon with them. I'm tempted to demand that she call in sick.

"Better?" she asks, and when I look up, I find a devilish grin, as if she can read my dirty thoughts.

A part of me wants to pull her down so I can kiss that grin right off her face. And then keep kissing her, because I couldn't get enough of that tongue last night, something that never happens.

But we don't have time for that, and I need to taste these pink nipples of hers.

I answer by leaning forward to seize one of them in my mouth and suck hard while I fit her other tit in my palm, squeezing it gently.

Mercy cries out, and I respond by twirling my tongue around the bud, my nose picking up that delicious floral scent against her skin. She smells incredible. She tastes even better.

Her fingers curl through the back of my hair, much gentler than she was with me last night. I don't mind either—rough or soft, I'll take whatever Mercy's willing to give me. I feel her curious eyes on me as I shift focus to her other nipple, flicking it with my tongue. "I'll spend more time with these later," I promise, reaching blindly for the foil packet. "But right now, I need your panties off."

Her gaze drops to where I'm holding my dick in my fist, and her chest caves with a sharp exhale. Slipping her thumbs beneath the elastic band of her white lace panties, she rolls her hips from one side to the other. She shimmies them off her ass and down her thighs until they're stretched too far to go farther down her parted legs. "Will this work for you—"

She squeals as I grab the backs of her thighs and hike her legs into the air until she loses her balance and falls back onto the table. I work her panties off the rest of the way, setting them on the table with her dress. I smile at the decadent view—Mercy's tight, smooth pussy, wet and at eye level, within easy reach of my mouth.

Leaning forward, I flatten and drag my tongue through her slit, savoring the sweet taste.

She lets out a deep, guttural moan, and her thighs fall apart. "Don't stop."

I chuckle. "You're going to be late for work."

"I won't take long, I swear." She's practically mewling as she stretches her slender arms over her head. "*Please*, Gabriel."

"*Fuck.*" I yank my T-shirt over my head and push her thighs apart until they won't go any wider. Then I dive in, letting my tongue roam every inch of her pussy before I focus on her clit, teasing her mercilessly. She cries out and bucks against my face. I love seeing this unguarded side of Mercy come out. I answer by pushing two fingers into her, her body clenching tightly around them as I begin pumping in and out, all while my tongue keeps playing with that bundle of nerves that'll make her scream my name.

When her fingers begin pawing at my hair, looking for purchase to grasp and pull, I know she's close. I abruptly pull away.

"No!" She pants, her back arched against the table, her beautiful tits in the air. "Don't stop. Please."

I chuckle as I stand and fit the condom on. "Sorry, baby. But the only way you're coming right now is with me inside you." Because I don't think I can listen to what I heard last night and *not* blow my load this time around.

God, she is fucking glorious, naked and flushed and writhing on the table beneath me, waiting for me as I lean over her splayed body. She peers up at me with that hooded, wild, sexed-up gaze. Waiting.

I can't believe this is happening. I'm not going to lose my chance though.

I line the tip of my cock up with her slick opening and begin pushing into her heat,

Her mouth falls open but no sound comes, her pussy molding itself to my hard flesh as I ever so slowly sink inside. "You are so tight. I've never felt a …" I let those words fade. *Talking about other women while you're in a woman is not cool, you idiot.*

"Stop chasing loose women then," Mercy throws back through gritted teeth, fire in her eyes as she glares up at me.

I groan, her angry streak only making my dick swell more. I pull out a bit and then try again, watching my cock sink deeper into her this time. She may be tight but she is *so* fucking wet. I'm not going to last more than thirty seconds.

I grab her hips and drag her body down, making it easier to fold myself over until we're chest to chest, forehead to forehead, her long lashes skimming mine, our ragged breaths a hot fog mixing together.

I capture her lips in mine, gliding my tongue into her mouth in a painfully slow dance. She responds in kind, matching my pace, the tip of her tongue dragging around the rim of my lips, tasting herself no doubt. The girl has skill. It makes me wonder what this mouth will do with my dick.

A burn starts coursing down my spine, and my balls tighten. Jesus, I'm going to come no matter if I move or not—

She seizes a fistful of my hair and tugs my head back. "Quit teasing and fuck me already," she whispers, nipping hard at my bottom lip with her teeth.

"Christ, woman." A deep sound escapes my throat. I

pull away to stand again. Grasping her splayed legs, I thrust hard into her, earning her loud cry.

"Sorry, what was that? What did you want me to do?" I say through clenched teeth.

"*Please,*" she moans, arching her back, one hand sliding down her belly to play with herself.

I hold the urge to remind her that she wasn't going to beg, and I push deeper into her until my cock is buried to the hilt and she's panting, her beautiful face contorted in a mask of pleasurable pain.

"You sure?"

"Yes." She bites her lip. "And, just so you know, this doesn't change anything between us. I still hate you."

I smile as I begin pumping into her, my hips pistoning in a hard, fast rhythm, her body jolting with each thrust, her creamy breasts swaying wildly. "Sure you do, baby. Nothing has changed at all."

Her fingernails claw at my hands where I've hooked them around her thighs before grasping my wrists and squeezing tight. Somehow I've managed to not blow my load in thirty seconds, but I doubt I'll pass the minute mark. Mercy just feels too damn good.

"I'm coming," she pants.

And ... I'm officially done.

I explode the second I feel the first muscle spasm around my dick. I'm forced to brace my body against the table with my hands as I ejaculate into her, her constricting muscles milking me dry.

"That ... was ..." Mercy's laughter is breathless as she lies splayed out on the table like a rag doll, a thin sheen of sweat coating her skin. "Don't you dare ruin this moment by saying something arrogant, Gabriel."

My name on this woman's lips will be my downfall.

And if not that, then this slick, tight pussy I'm buried in, that I'm not ready to leave. I'm still hard. A few minutes and a quick condom switch and I'd gladly continue. I check my watch. And curse.

"Yeah. I know." Mercy sighs as if she's as disappointed as I am.

I smooth my hands up her silky legs, drawing them up to settle on my shoulders. "We'll have all night tonight, I promise." I press my lips against her calf. *And tomorrow … and the next night …*

Her eyes trail the gentle kiss curiously, but she says nothing.

———

THE CLOCK on the dash reads 1:17 p.m. when I pull into the center's parking lot, my SUV bumping over the cracks in the pavement. "Only two minutes late."

Mercy smooths her dress over her lap and then fixes her bra strap. She's checking for anything out of place. Anything that might signal she spent her lunch hour naked on a table.

"Don't worry. Everyone will know you just got properly fucked."

She shoots at glare at me and then flips the visor down to rub a finger over her slightly swollen lips.

"Relax." I reach over to smooth my hand over her thick mane of hair where it looks out of place.

She heaves a sigh. "I should go." She collects the bag by her feet, the lunch I didn't give her the chance to eat. "So, I guess I'll see you later, after my class." She reaches for the door handle.

Before I realize what I'm doing, I grab hold of her arm, pulling her close to me. When she turns to question me, I lay a soft kiss against her lips.

She wears a deep frown when we part.

I chuckle. "What's wrong?"

"Nothing. I just …" She hesitates.

I arch my eyebrow. "Mercy?"

"You're just different than I thought you'd be."

In some ways. "I told you I was."

"Right. Well …" She swallows and her gaze flickers to my lips. "I'll see you later." She pauses, and then leans in to steal another kiss. "And this doesn't mean that I like you now."

"Of course not." I smirk. "But it probably means I'm going to get these beautiful lips around my cock tonight."

I catch the beginnings of a smile before she stifles it. "You wish." She escapes out the door, a mutter of, "Asshole," trailing behind her.

I watch her hips sway all the way into the building.

Great. I get to spend my afternoon with a raging hard-on.

29 MERCY

When I pull up to Gabriel's house that night after school, I'm fueled by nervous energy and my own stubbornness.

I was weak today. Arrogant Gabriel? I have no problem refusing that bastard. But that softer, more human version sitting beside me at lunch, the one so concerned about what I thought happened last night—I don't have enough armor to keep that one's appeal at bay. I— very stupidly— spent the afternoon convincing myself that today's sex break with Gabriel would be a one-time deal, and yet in my gut I already know that's not likely to be the case. Especially if he keeps pulling moves like the one when he dropped me off at work, when he kissed me goodbye so sweetly.

This man has invaded my life.

It isn't enough that he has lingered in my thoughts all afternoon and into the evening, distracting me, but I can still *feel* him—his heated gaze on my flesh, his firm grip on my hips, his hard length thrusting into me. I've caught myself wondering what unrushed sex, in a bed—all night long—might be like, and just the thought of that has fed this simmering ache between my legs for hours.

But there is no way in hell I'm about to let him think that my body is now his to do with whatever, whenever he wants.

The silver Mercedes SUV I remember from yesterday is parked in the driveway, along with a girlish sky-blue Z3 that I don't recall. Great. Caleb must be entertaining again. Next to him, Gabriel is beginning to look like an angel.

Collecting my bags from the back seat, I brace myself for whatever depravity I'm about to walk into and head inside. Thankfully, they're all just watching the baseball game on the big screen TV, clothed. Well … relatively. Caleb and the brawny twins from yesterday are all shirtless and pacing around the sectional, beers in hand, their focus on the man up to bat. Two beautiful brunettes I don't recognize are in cut-off jean shorts and bikini tops.

"Welcome home, honey." Caleb grins around a sip of his beer, his playful gaze doing a full head-to-toe scan of my body. "How was your day?"

"Fine," I say in a polite but flat tone. He did flash and proposition me this morning, after all.

The twin to his left clears his throat.

"Oh, you didn't meet Finn yesterday, did you?" Caleb asks with a mock frown.

"Not officially." *Though I'm well acquainted with what he*

sounds like when he comes. I feel my cheeks heat as I meet the twin's gaze. "Hi."

Finn strolls forward, offering me his hand and a broad smile. I push aside the fact that that hand was holding a woman's head down while she blew him and accept the friendly gesture. He's handsome and a mirror of his twin brother—both of them with brilliant hazel-green eyes and dark hair and muscle padding their chest and arms. If not for the other brother's beard, I'd have no hope of telling them apart.

"That's my brother, Felix. Sorry, I didn't catch your name," he says in a smooth voice.

"It's Mercy," I admit with reluctance. *And three … two …*

"Mercy." Finn's green eyes sparkle. "Is that, like, your stage name?"

The brunettes on the couch titter as if that's the funniest, most original thing they've ever heard.

I roll my eyes.

"It's her name," comes Gabriel's deep voice from somewhere unseen, sounding out of breath. He appears a second later from around the corner, shirtless and holding a towel, his brown hair a damp, sexy mess, his trunks wet and clinging to his muscular frame. My stomach does a flip as I admire the way the elastic band sits low on his waist, showing off that gorgeous vee of his hips.

Gabriel looks downright edible.

And I still can't believe I had sex with this scoundrel over lunch. On a table in his club, no less.

It's not happening again.

It's not happening again.

It's not happening again.

The lustful gleam in his Gabriel's eyes steals my breath. That look says something entirely different. It's saying he thinks we'll be doing it again in about five minutes.

Heat stirs between my legs.

"Hey, Gabriel," the girl on the left croons in a seductive voice. "Are you going to come hang out with us now—"

"No." He doesn't even look at her, stopping in front of me.

Is it wrong, how much I enjoy him shutting her down? Maybe, but I'm brimming with vindictive joy right now. Though, I'm also wondering how many times he *hasn't* shut her down in the past.

His gaze flickers to my mouth, but he doesn't move in to kiss me. He's waiting for me to make the first move, I realize.

I merely arch an "as if" eyebrow at him. His responding chuckle sends a warm shiver down my spine.

"Rosita made carnitas. You hungry?" he asks with a dimple-filled smile.

"I grabbed something on campus. But thanks." I feel my own responding smile stretch my lips, unbidden. If there's one thing about being Gabriel's somewhat-captive, it's that I won't starve. He's always feeding me or trying to feed me. It's as if he's actually capable of caring about anyone but himself.

And I need to nip these thoughts in the bud. "I have an assignment I need to work on, so I'm going to go and

…" My words drift as Gabriel slides my bags off my shoulder.

"You should get started on that right away then." Curling his arm around my waist, he swivels us around and steers us out of the living room, toward the hall that leads to his bedroom, carrying my things in his free hand.

He isn't wasting any time.

Flutters stir in my stomach. That firm resolution to deny him sex tonight? The one I was so adamant on five minutes ago? It's already on shaky ground.

"I was just telling Mercy how much you like to share with your big brother," Caleb calls out.

"Not a chance in hell. And put some fucking pants on in the mornings from now on so she doesn't have to see your limp dick," Gabriel throws back without missing a beat. We round the corner to the sounds of laughter.

"How did you know about that?"

"Because it's Caleb."

I swallow. "And is it true?" It's crystal clear what his brother is implying.

Gabriel opens his mouth but hesitates. When he finally chooses his words, they're sharp, almost a warning. "He's not laying a hand or any other part of himself on you."

Interesting. But he didn't deny sharing other women with his brother, I note.

"Did you get your assignment in?" he asks casually, as if he's *not* leading me into the bedroom for the sole purpose of fucking me.

"Barely. Every printer in the library was being used when I got there and I had to wait. I was late for class." I clear the shakiness from my voice. I'm suddenly nervous.

Gabriel scowls. "Why didn't you use the printer here, in the office?"

"I just … I didn't know," I murmur as he ushers me into the bedroom, pushing the door shut behind us. We were on very different terms last night. I'm unclear on what terms we're on now.

His big body closes in on me, herding me backward until I'm pressed up against the wall. "I told you to use anything you want in this house." He dips his face into the crook of my neck.

I close my eyes and shudder as his lips skate over my skin. How do I deny this? It feels so damn good and there's no risk of my emotions getting tangled up, because I hate Gabriel Easton. Or at least, I strongly dislike *everything* he stands for. When he's being like this though …

He lays a soft, tongue-tipped kiss just below my earlobe that I somehow feel all the way down to my pebbled nipples. "Use *everything*, including my dick, which is incredibly hard right now." He leans in to press the proof of that statement against my stomach.

"Your dick is *always* hard," I managed through a breathy laugh. "And your shorts are cold."

"Sorry. I was doing laps." He shucks his wet trunks and kicks them away, leaving himself gloriously naked in front of me. "Better?"

I release a soft gasp in admiration, my fingertips dragging over his taut stomach, itching to reach down and wrap my hand around his length. I haven't so much as grazed a finger over that cock yet.

His muscles clench under my touch. "Hold that thought," he whispers, his hands moving to the zipper on the back of my dress.

There are a few seconds—a fuzzy moment in the back of my mind—where I tell myself I should tell him to stop, but as he drags the zipper down, the words never form on my tongue.

He pushes the short sleeves down off my shoulders, and the material slips off to pool at my ankles, leaving me in my bra and panties. He drags his fingertips up the inside of my thigh.

"Wait." I clamp my legs together, stalling his fingers just before they dip into my panties. "I need a shower."

"No you don't." His free hand unfastens my bra clasp. He pulls it off and bends over to catch one of my nipples between his teeth, teasing it gently before sucking it into his mouth, eliciting a soft moan from my lips.

"I *do*. I didn't have one this morning."

"Hmm ..." Dropping to his knees, he presses his face into the apex of my thighs. "You smell great to me, but let me have a taste."

Jesus Christ. "I need a shower," I repeat more firmly, squeezing his hands, stopping them before they succeed in pulling my panties off.

His dark, hooded eyes lock on mine as he sucks my clit through my panties. A tremble runs through my body. If he keeps that up, I'm going to come. "Gabriel ..."

"Okay."

I squirm out of his grasp, feeling his gaze on my ass the entire way to the bathroom, until I push the door shut.

I shake my head at myself. "You couldn't last five minutes in a room with him."

The walk-in shower in Gabriel's private bath is luxury at its finest, with two separate spray heads from the ceiling and another three affixed to the wall, along with a built-in bench on once side. It could easily fit three adults in it.

I don't doubt Gabriel has taken advantage of that on more than one occasion.

Pushing that thought aside, I slip off my panties and step into the stall, fumbling with the various dials until there's a steady stream of hot water coming from the head on the far left. And I think about that man out there in the bedroom, waiting for me. He's screwed a lot of women, he's admitted that much to me. I really don't know anything about him beyond the things I'd rather not know—his corrupt father, the club he runs that was likely bought with drug money, and this playboy lifestyle that he and his brother lead. But what about everything *else*? Did he go to college? Has he ever been in love? What happened to his mother? Does he even like his father?

I'm probably better not knowing anything about Gabriel, I accept, standing beneath the stream, pushing my hands through my hair to wet it. Knowing those details makes him human, which makes him someone I could care about. Gabriel is not the kind of man I want to care about. I just need to ride this out until the end of the week—

The stall door slides open, and in strolls Gabriel.

"You weren't kidding." My gaze flits over his jutting erection as my excitement swells.

He turns the other dials, and in seconds, warm water is streaming from all showerheads, filling the sizeable shower with steam. He settles onto the bench, muscular thighs splayed, his magnificent body on display.

"You won't even let me shower alone?" I can't seem to bring my usual bitterness to my voice.

"Don't mind me." He leans back against the tiled wall and wraps his fist around the base of that big, beautiful cock. He strokes himself slowly.

"Don't worry, I won't." I turn my back to him and pretend that the sight doesn't faze me. Meanwhile my core is throbbing. It reminds me of my dream last night, and the thought of straddling his lap right now makes me want to rush my shower.

But he's banking on that. That's what he's used to— girls like those in the living room, batting their eyes and crooning "oh Gabriel, come hang out with me!" right before they joke about blowing him as a means to *actually* blowing him.

I am not one of them and he needs to remember that.

My showers are normally fifteen minutes long but now that he's here, I'm going to take my sweet-ass time. I dump a glob of my shampoo into my palm and massage it into my roots at a scalp-massage slow pace.

"What is that scent?" Gabriel asks in a low, husky voice.

"Rose petals." It's been my favorite scent for as long as I can remember, and my only splurge in life.

He inhales deeply. "Your skin smells like that, too."

"That's because my body wash is from the same line."

"I love the smell of you. Of *every* square inch of you."

A flash of his face between my legs hits me then, and my thighs tighten. I fight the urge to steal a glance over my shoulder, and continue cleaning my hair instead, working up a thick lather.

"Mercy." His voice sounds pained. "You almost finished?"

"Do I *look* almost finished?" It comes out sounding bitchy, but I resist the urge to follow it up with a more soothing response.

"It looks like you're trying to torture me."

Bingo.

"I need those lips of yours on this."

He doesn't need to elaborate on what *this* is. My mouth waters at the thought of sucking him off, but I'm not about to make it easy for him. I school my voice. "Well, I'm busy right now. You'll just have to wait. Or find someone else to do it for you."

The second those words leave my mouth, I want to pull them back. We both know there are two women sitting in this house at this very moment who would be willing to suck his dick, and if Gabriel calls my bluff, I'll either have to relent or taunt him to go.

I don't want to relent. But if he leaves and goes to one of them … My stomach tightens. I'm jealous, I realize. Jealous of the idea of him being with another woman.

I hold my breath, waiting for the challenge that's no doubt coming.

But Gabriel surprises me with "I'll wait."

I let out a long, soft sigh of relief, and hope he doesn't catch it. But then I casually add, "Just so you know, that's not a guarantee of anything after I'm done with my shower." *Oh Lord, Mercy, you really are testing him—and yourself—tonight.*

He doesn't respond.

I take my sweet time beneath the showerhead, rinsing out the sudsy shampoo until every last bit is down the drain.

"You have an incredible ass," he says as I reach for my conditioner.

"Thanks?" I slowly work a quarter-sized amount through the ends of my long hair.

"Have you ever let anyone fuck it?"

"No."

"Will you let me?"

Heat floods between my legs, and the instant denial I've given others who've asked dies on my lips. I've never understood the appeal. I've certainly never felt the desire. It just seemed dirty. But in Gabriel's world, where *everything* seems dirty, I'm more curious than anything. He's certainly alluded to it a few times already, and my guess is he knows what he's doing. And then there was that quick tease with his tongue last night …

I finally settle on, "I haven't agreed to letting you do *anything* again."

"Tell me you're done with your shower." There's a slightly pained inflection in his gravelly voice.

My lower belly tenses, the urge to feel him inside me again, to watch him lose control, threatening to overpower my will. But instead I reach for my loofah and, squirting body wash on it, begin working it into a lather over my arms. "Nope."

He's behind me in seconds. "You're torturing me," he growls, his lips pressed against my ear, his breathing ragged.

"Maybe," I admit, reveling in the feel of his naked body looming so close behind me, his jutting erection resting against my back. "But I still have to wash my body."

He seizes the loofah from my grip and begins rubbing it over my skin, quickly making his way from my arm to my collarbone, to my torso, to my breasts, his fingertips catching my beaded nipples with each circular pass.

"You know I have other body parts that need cleaning, too," I tease, my voice trembling slightly now. It's getting harder to resist the urge to grind my hips back into his waiting body.

He solves that problem for me by roping his other arm around my body and pulling me back flush against him. His lips find my neck just as his callused hand cups a breast with a gentle squeeze. "You mean my favorite part?" He slides the loofah downward to settle between my legs.

I answer by parting my thighs a touch. Okay, maybe one night of sex with Gabriel *and then* that's it. Today *was* rushed.

"That's it, baby, open up for me," he purrs into my ear. I've never liked terms of endearment, but for some reason, anything that comes out of this man's mouth is quickly becoming acceptable to me. I adjust my stance further, giving him plenty of room to fit his hand in between. He begins stroking back and forth.

I turn to capture his lips with mine. He licks along the seam of my mouth and somehow I feel it all the way between my legs. He knows how to use his tongue like no other man I've ever met, and just the memory of it against my clit earlier has me parting my thighs even farther.

The moment his tongue slips into my mouth, I give it a hard suck.

"Holy *fuck*, Mercy. You're killing me," he pushes out through gritted teeth, thrusting his swollen length against my back.

I pull back just enough to meet his gaze. "Then I guess you better get me off fast." It's a soft demand, delivered with a wicked smile.

His jaw tightens as he stares down hard at me, that dark storm brewing within the depths of his gaze. And I have to wonder how Gabriel Easton reacts when he's *this* riled up and a woman demands her own pleasure before his. Has anyone ever dared do it before?

Have I just finally pushed him too far?

He tosses the sponge to the tiled floor and, grabbing

my hips, spins me around. His body looms as he herds me backward until I'm pressed against the tile wall and out of the stream of water. "You want me to get you off?" A vindictive smirk curls his lips, making my stomach twist with nerves. "Okay, Mercy, I'll get you off."

He reaches for a bottle on the shelf.

"What is that?" I ask warily.

"Something to help me get you off, *fast.*" He flips the cap and squeezes the bottle. Clear liquid pours out in globs.

Gabriel has lube at the ready in his shower?

I'll likely be repulsed by that later, but right now I'm throbbing for a release. Still …

I lick my lips. "I don't think I need that."

He chuckles as he sets the bottle back in its place. "Let me worry about what you need." He makes a point of spreading the clear, slippery liquid across *all* of his fingers.

My inner muscles clench in anticipation.

His free hand fists my hair at my nape and gently tugs my head back until our eyes meet. Fire burns in his. "Trust me, you're going to enjoy this," he whispers. A gasp slips from me as he slides three fingers into my entrance all at once, my body providing no resistance against the intrusion. He follows it with a swirl of his thumb against my clit that makes my knees threaten to buckle. My hands reach for his powerful shoulders as I brace myself.

"I've got you," he murmurs, still gripping my hair, his eyes locked on mine.

I catch the wicked gleam in them a second before a finger prods my tight entrance. I automatically tense.

"Relax," he coaxes, his whisper low and grating.

I take a deep breath, willing my body to listen. The second it does, that slick pinkie of his is slipping past the tight ring of muscle. With its intrusion comes a slight burn.

"Let's give your body a minute to adjust." He presses a light kiss on my lips as his thumb continues toying with my clit.

I shamelessly explore his body with my hands while we wait, admiring the many hard curves that make this man physically beautiful beyond compare. I slide my palms over his chiseled torso, cup the padded muscle over his chest, stroke his round nipples with the pads of my thumbs, revel in the strength of his shapely biceps.

My hands have settled on his broad shoulders again when I meet his gaze. His eyes have a strange and unde-cipherable look in them. Almost morose.

I frown. "What's wrong?"

It's a few beats before he responds. "Nothing." His grip on my hair tightens again. "Look at me. Don't stop looking at me," he demands as he begins working his fingers in and out of my body, slowly at first but quickly picking up speed, until he's deep inside me with each thrust and my clit is tingling with the promise of an orgasm. That slight burn has been replaced with the oddly erotic feel of Gabriel claiming me in an incredibly intimate, private way.

His eyes glow with his own need, and yet he keeps tending to mine, the muscles in his working arm cording tightly, and I can't tell if it's the lube or my arousal that has made me so wet but it's definitely working to my advantage.

His lips curl. "You like me being in there, don't you?"

It feels weird and invasive and … yes, I do. "Not as much as you do," I say instead, in a breathy pant as I start rolling my hips, riding his hand.

"Christ, Mercy," he groans. "I'm going to blow my load on my own if you don't hurry up." His pace and pressure pick up, stirring that familiar heat that blooms through my core.

All it takes is a glance down at the way his forearm tenses with exertion. "I'm coming," I choke out as the first ripples hit me and then I can't control my cries. I ride Gabriel's hand as waves of intense pleasure hit me. When they finally fade, I'm left clinging to his shoulders and my legs are trembling.

He gives one last teasing stroke against my clit and then gently slips his fingers out, leaving me feeling oddly empty. "Mercy." He takes my hand in his and presses it against his velvety smooth length. His cock is long and thick and hard against my palm. And the idea of having it between my thighs again brings a fresh flood of wet heat straight to my center. "Don't make me wait anymore," he whispers, his voice strangled. "I've been waiting all day for you."

Something stirs deep inside me at that candid confession. Gabriel so freely admits it; his usual arrogant demeanor is nowhere to be seen and has barely made itself known all day.

I stroke him once, ever so slowly. The responding guttural moan that escapes his throat makes me abandon all thought of torturing him any longer.

I drop to my knees in front of him. The shower tile is hard but I ignore it because my guess is he's not going to last long, not the way his chest is heaving with his ragged breaths. His eyes burn bright with arousal as he watches me lick my lips once, and they flare as I run my tongue up the underside of his shaft. The view of Gabriel's body from this angle is enough to make my body ache for another orgasm, but there's time for that later. For now, I'm shocked at how excited I am to do this.

I wrap my fist around his base and swirl my tongue around his tip a few times, savoring the salty drops that have leaked out, before I take him in for the first time, stretching my mouth as wide as I can around his girth. Holy hell, he's *big*.

"It's okay, baby, take your time to get used to me," he croons, gently pushing my wet, clingy hair off my forehead, nothing but concern in his tone and on his face. He's already assumed I'm not experienced. I should be annoyed, but all I am is amused.

"Aww, are you worried about me?" I tease, adjusting the angle. I press a sweet kiss against his tip, cast him a wink, and then dive in, taking his full length in one fell swoop until it hits the back of my throat.

Gabriel chokes out a curse as I ease off him, only to quickly come down again, letting my lips suction over him, savoring the way his cock fills my throat.

"Mercy," he cries, his head falling back as his fingers

weave through my hair, still slick from conditioner.

I press my palms against his hips to keep control just as he adjusts his stance and rocks his hips. His eyes blaze as he watches me blow him, his fist tightening its grip in my hair, his lips parting as his breathing becomes ragged. He's muttering something unintelligible, though I catch my name more than once. I ignore him, suctioning my mouth over his dick as I bob up and down.

I don't even have to pretend to enjoy this.

He explodes without warning and much sooner than I expected, filling my mouth, his legs shaking, his deep moans reverberating through the shower stall. When the last pulse dies down, I slip off him and lean over to discreetly spit down the drain before climbing to my feet.

Gabriel's face is a mask of bewilderment. "You are … That was …" His dark gaze sears my lips as he pants out his breaths, unable to get his full thoughts out for whatever reason.

"Don't worry, baby, just take your time to get used to me," I tease in a mocking voice. "Maybe next time, you'll last longer."

His eyebrows arch. "Oh, you think you're funny, do you?" He lurches forward, sandwiching my body between himself and the tile. He grabs the backs of my thighs and lifts me, guiding my legs around his hips.

I feel the urge to wrap my arms around his neck and so I do, pulling him closer, my pebbled nipples grazing his firm chest. Pleasant shivers course through my body.

"You want to see how long I can last?" he taunts,

adjusting his stance. The tip of his cock prods against my opening as he lays a searing kiss against my lips.

Jesus. He's still rock hard.

"Condom," I remind him.

He groans.

"Gabriel …"

"Fuck, I don't have one in here." With a second, louder groan, he loops a strong arm around my waist and pulls away from the wall. I cling to his powerful body as he pushes open the shower stall door and storms out. In the back of my mind I'm conscious that we've left all the showerheads running and that the air is so much colder now and that I still have conditioner in my hair and we're dripping wet, but none of that matters as Gabriel carries me out of the bathroom and straight for his bed. I'm more in awe of how good he feels, how addicted I am to this body of his, how much I want him inside me again.

Still holding me with one arm as if my weight is nothing at all, he fishes a condom out of his nightstand and tears the foil packet with his teeth. Kneeling down onto the bed, he leans over to release me onto the mattress, where I flop and wait, legs spread, watching with rapt attention as he rolls the condom on.

"Where were we …" He fits himself between my legs, adjusting his crushing weight as he lies down on top of me. Collecting my hands, he raises my arms above my head, pinning them down, his fingers weaving through mine. His muscular arms form a cocoon around my head as he leans in to press a slow, tantalizing kiss against my lips.

I wasn't expecting missionary style with Gabriel, but I can already tell it's going to be the most erotic position I've ever experienced.

"I think you had to prove something to me?" I whisper sweetly, stretching my thighs wider for him. We're both shivering slightly, though I doubt that will last long.

"Oh yeah." That one-sided dimpled smirk kicks in as I feel his head prodding my opening again. And with a single, hard thrust, he's buried deep inside me.

I cry out at being stretched so far, so quickly.

"I'll bet you're not regretting all that lube now." He eases himself out almost fully, only to thrust in hard again.

I gasp as he fills me, the intensity of it almost too much.

His lips settle on that spot below my ear again—it's clearly a favorite of his and is quickly becoming mine—and he kisses me slowly, teasing my skin with the tip of his tongue as he gently rolls his hips, allowing me to get used to his size.

"I could live in here all day long."

I could let him, I admit silently. I clench my inner muscles around his cock, earning his growl. And yet he continues at that slow, punishing pace, his sculpted body flexing as he thrusts into me again and again and again.

He chokes out a curse as moisture floods my core. "That's for me, isn't it?" His hooded gaze meets mine and the look in it is searing. His hip rolls quickly turn into plunges, the pace picking up. I meet each one, my hips rocking, my legs spreading wider, my hands straining against his grip, desperate to roam his powerful body. But he doesn't release them from his grip, swirling his thumbs across my palms in slow circles instead. His gaze shifts to study my lips, and then we're kissing, our mouths working against each other in a messy tangle of lips and tongues and nips as if we can't get close enough.

Michelle once described in detail what taking ecstasy is like—how all your senses are overstimulated, how you can feel a charge in every square inch of your body, how you long to be touched and need to touch others.

If that's all true, then sex with Gabriel is nothing short of ecstasy, because every square inch of me right now feels utter bliss. Every inch of me revels in this connection with him. It's not long before that familiar tingle builds in my spine. I pull my legs up higher, needing Gabriel deeper inside me when I orgasm.

"You're coming," he pants, and it's not a question. Not that he needs to ask; he can read my urgent squirms and my ragged breaths for what they are.

I bite his bottom lip in answer because that's what seemed to set him off in the past. It works again as his strokes speed up, as he hikes one of his knees up to adjust his position and give him more purchase. He thrusts hard into me, pushing in so deep that I'm crying out each time, the intensity *almost* painful.

My orgasm surges through my body.

"Fuck!" Gabriel cries out a second before I feel his release inside me, my muscles clench against it, draining him of every drop, until Gabriel's large body quivers atop me, spent.

Our heavy pants fill the otherwise quiet bedroom.

"The bed is soaked. I'll need to change the sheets," I murmur absently, reveling in the weight of him draped over me, his head nestled against mine. His hands are still entwined with mine.

He chuckles, and it's such a lovely sound. I feel it through every inch. I feel it deep inside me where he's still buried. It makes me smile. It makes me lean in and press a lazy kiss against his soft lips.

"I can't last with you," he admits. "The second I hear you come, I'm done for."

"Sorry."

Another chuckle. Another tickle deep inside. "You don't sound sorry."

"I'm not."

A reluctant sound escapes him. "I guess we should shut off the shower."

"I still have conditioner in my hair."

He inhales. "Leave it in. I love that smell."

"It'll still smell good, but I need it out or my hair will be slimy."

"Just like another part of you right now."

I cringe. "I'm not *slimy* down there!"

"No, your pussy isn't slimy," he agrees. "In fact, I'll happily shove my tongue in it right now."

My inner muscles clench in response to his dirty talk.

He groans. "Don't do that unless you're ready to be fucked again."

I am. I bite back that answer. "I really do have an assignment to finish."

With a heavy sigh, he releases my hands as he climbs

off me, stealing a quick suck on one of my nipples and then pausing to study the view intently. The man seems to worship my body.

And I'm all for that.

Wrapping the used condom in a tissue and tossing it in the nearby trash, he swoops in to lift me off the bed and carry me back to the shower the same way he brought me out, my legs wrapped around his hips and my arms coiled around his neck.

The warm spray beneath the jets is soothing. I expect Gabriel to abandon me now that he's gotten what he wanted, but he stays. "Your hair *is* slimy." He works the conditioner out of it with his fingers, a slight cringe twisting his face.

"So is your semen," I throw back.

He grins. And then hesitates as if remembering something. "You didn't swallow."

"You noticed that, did you?"

"I did." A vicious smile curls his lips. "You won't do it?"

"Not if I don't know where the guy has been." Not that *not* swallowing would make much difference, if he does have any sexually transmitted diseases. I guess it's more a psychological thing on my part.

"I'm clean, Mercy. I get tested regularly."

I let out an unattractive snort as I work the rest of the conditioner out. "Yeah, contrary to what guys think, that doesn't inspire confidence. You've probably fucked half of Phoenix."

Whatever retort he had coming dies on his lips. "Fine. I'll get tested again tomorrow."

"What's the point? It'll take days for the results, and I'm only here until this weekend anyway."

A deep frown furrows his forehead.

"That was the deal, remember?" I remind him. "You said you wouldn't go back on it." Four more days of this. Though *this* is turning out be not so bad after all.

"No. I won't." He shakes his head absently, his thoughts off somewhere far away. He leans in to kiss me, his lips moving tantalizingly slow. I find myself sinking into his hard body, my fingers weaving through his hair as my arms curl around his head.

Who knew Gabriel could kiss like this? *Would* kiss like this, with a woman he propositioned so callously in the prison parking lot.

Maybe I'm all wrong about him.

He pries his lips off mine. "What if we make a new deal?"

"What do you mean?" My heart skips a beat even as my wariness sparks. "You said you'd protect my father for good—"

"That's not changing." He pulls his bottom lip between his teeth in thought. "What if I hire him a lawyer. One that's good enough to get him an appeal."

Blood races in my ears. I could get him out of there. I could get this bullshit conviction overturned. "Are you kidding me?"

"No, I'm not." I see the seriousness in his eyes. "Is that something you'd be interested in?"

I bite my tongue before I blurt out the yes I want to say. "Why would you want to do that? You're already getting what you want from me."

He shrugs in a nonchalant way, but I can tell it's forced. "Maybe a week of fucking you isn't enough. Maybe I need longer."

My breath catches. I was not expecting this.

"How long would be enough?" I hear myself ask. I can't believe I'm considering this.

His jaw tenses. "I'll let you know."

Oh my God, oh my God, oh my God. What am I signing up for? "We'd have to discuss terms."

"Of course." He smiles and those devilish dimples pop. "You and your terms."

Wait a minute. Jesus. "I don't know, Gabriel."

"What don't you know," he says evenly, his fingers stroking up and down my arm in a soothing manner. "We're both enjoying this. I can help you; let me help you."

I *am* enjoying this. Too much. But this is basically prostitution—sex with Gabriel in exchange for lawyer's fees.

Sex with a man who likely sells drugs.

I swallow my rising panic. "Yes, but you know my history. With my mother. And I know enough about your father. And likely you." *And the dirty empire you thrive on.*

"And I told you that I'm not my father."

"So, are you saying that you *aren't* selling drugs?" I ask carefully. Would that really change things for me? I'm still basically prostituting myself!

His jaw tenses. "That's what I'm saying."

It's the first time he's ever outright denied it.

And the instant reaction in my gut—that sudden,

overwhelming relief—confirms that it *does* matter to me.

If it's true.

"I want to believe you," I whisper.

"Then believe me." He brushes strands of hair off my forehead. "I'll let you finish your shower."

"How considerate of you." My voice drips with sarcasm. This shower should have ended half an hour ago. We've wasted a lot of water while *not* showering.

It's too steamy to admire his naked form as he leaves. I settle on closing my eyes and bringing up my vivid memory as I rinse out my conditioner.

Another lawyer for my father. A good, expensive lawyer. It would mean I don't have to follow through with this idiotic plan of mine for law school.

But why is Gabriel willing to pay for this? I don't get it. He could have any woman he wants. Ten of them, all at once. So what is it about *me* that has him making these outrageous offers that he knows I can't refuse?

Something tells me he's going to require more than another week in his bed this time around.

If I'm being totally honest with myself, that's quickly becoming less of a punishment.

But if my father ever found out about any of this … I clutch my stomach against the dread that stirs with the thought. He'd refuse the lawyer on sight. I'll have to concoct some big lie. I hate lying to him, but I'll gladly do it to get him out of there.

Hope begins to blossom in my chest, even as I wonder if I've gone absolutely mad for considering another deal with Gabriel.

The angel who has fallen far from grace.

30 GABRIEL

THE SOUND of skin slapping against skin and female moans don't deter me from banging on Caleb's bedroom door once before throwing it open. "Can you take five and come downstairs?"

"Are you fucking kidding me? I'm kind of busy right now." He gestures at the naked brunette riding his cock. The other one is equally naked and spread out at the end of his bed, playing with herself while waiting her turn. I guess Felix and Finn have taken their dicks and gone elsewhere.

"We need to talk. *Now.*"

"All I need is five. Why don't you get with Mindy—"

"Misty!" she corrects haughtily, but then flashes a seductive smile and swivels her body and spreads her legs wide, showing off her wares.

My dick doesn't so much as twitch.

And, shit, how would this look if Mercy were to walk in here right now? I shouldn't be in this bedroom.

My stomach fills with dread. Jesus Christ. What has that woman done to me? She officially owns me.

"Meet me downstairs in five. This is serious. It's about our talk from earlier."

With that I bolt out of there and head for the one place in our house that we know we can talk safely. I punch the eight-digit code into the door and slip inside to cellar, immediately regretting not pulling more than a pair of shorts on as goose bumps erupt all over my bare chest in the temperature-controlled room. Thankfully, I don't have to wait long. Not even a minute later, Caleb is pushing through the door, dressed in boxers. The heavy door slams shut behind us.

He throws his hands in the air. "What the hell is going on?"

"I want out of the H. Completely. I want no ties to it. No laundering. Nothing."

"Yeah …" Caleb frowns like he's not understanding. "That's what we've been talking about all along—"

"No, I mean, I want out of it now. *Today.*" I begin pacing up and down the narrow space, lined on either side with rows upon rows of hundreds of thousands of dollars' worth of wines from all over the world.

"What's the sudden rush?"

I sigh. "Mercy."

His eyebrows raise.

"I don't want her finding out."

"I thought she already figured it out."

"No, she *thinks* all this"—I gesture outwards—"was bought with drug money."

"Because it *was.*"

"But she doesn't *know* that. She only *thinks* it. And knowing and thinking are two different things."

"Semantics."

"If we can get away from it all and go totally legit, I won't be lying. Not totally."

He glares at me. "Is she a complete airhead?"

"No, man. She's smart." Sexy-ass smart. "But I just told her we're not into that business."

"So you lied."

"Yes. *Technically.*"

"Jesus, Gabe." He rubs his hands over his face. "You made me abandon two pussies for this."

"They'll be waiting for you when you get back."

He nods reluctantly. Those two would camp outside with the coyotes if it meant riding either of our dicks tonight. "So you're actually into her?"

"I don't know." All I know is the moment she reminded me that she'll be leaving at the end of her week, that this thing between us isn't real, my mind started spinning with ways to keep her longer, to *make* it real. I need time to get to know her. I need time for her to get to know me, to decide she can't live without me. "Yes. I'm into her. Fuck!" I've been a tight wire all afternoon, counting down the hours until she got home. Back there in the shower? I was ready to fall to my knees and beg her to let me touch her. I don't know what the hell is happening to me, but ever since last night, she has been wedged into my brain. Everything revolves around her.

Including my conscience, apparently.

"We need to meet with Merrick and Vince Perri. Figure out where their heads are at." My conversation with them at Empire last night was guarded and vague. What I did gather from it is that they have no interest in following in the family drug business either.

Caleb's already shaking his head. "We can't trust them. Do I need to remind you what they did to our mother?"

"Merrick and Vince had nothing to do with that. They were our age."

"Still ... I don't like this. And if Dad ever caught wind—"

"He's not gonna hear shit about it."

"*If he did* catch wind, we're as good as dead. You don't think he wouldn't put a hit on his own sons? Think again." Caleb's pacing now, too. "Can't you just tell her the truth and take what comes? I don't know, maybe you can convince her that her job is a way to absolve any guilt she has over being with you."

"She's not an idiot. Plus, her mom OD'd on heroin, so she'll never go for it."

"Are you—" He barks out with bitter laughter. "Sorry, it's *not* funny but it's fucking funny. Honestly, of *all* the women you had to pick up at Fulcort."

I groan. "Tell me about it." But Mercy isn't like any other woman I've ever met. I don't really know her, but I *need* to get to know her. If she'll stay long enough.

"I'll say one thing. I've never seen you so motivated by pussy." He stops his frantic pacing suddenly and snorts. "I'm getting you a T-shirt."

I punch him hard in the arm.

"Fuck!" He winces and rubs the spot. "Okay, so say we distance ourselves from Dad's world. Go totally legit.

You honestly think she'd actually want to be with your sorry ass if you weren't baiting her?"

"Yes." The way she looked up at me, the way she kisses me … She may not know it yet, but we belong together. That or I'm a fucking maniac. One or the other. "You let me worry about that." Bait is exactly what I dangled in front of her before I got out of the shower. The idea hit me as I was kissing her, and I barely gave it second's thought before blurting it out.

The way her eyes lit up before her conscience kicked into high gear tells me I hit the mark.

I can't imagine what kind of terms she'll come up with, but I'll agree to anything that woman requests as long as it means she's not leaving my bed anytime soon.

Mercy will be mine.

———

Did you enjoy Sweet Mercy?
If so, please consider leaving a review.

ALSO BY K.A. TUCKER

The Wolf Hotel Series:

Tempt Me (#1)

Break Me (#2)

Teach Me (#3)

Surrender To Me (#4)

Empire Nightclub Series:

Sweet Mercy (#1)

Gabriel Fallen (#2)

Dirty Empire (#3)

Fallen Empire (#4)

For Contemporary Romance, Women's Fiction, and
Romantic Suspense by K.A. Tucker, visit katuckerbooks.com

ABOUT THE AUTHOR

K.A. Tucker writes captivating stories with an edge.

She is the internationally bestselling author of the Ten Tiny Breaths and Burying Water series, He Will Be My Ruin, Until It Fades, Keep Her Safe, The Simple Wild, Be the Girl, and Say You Still Love Me. Her books have been featured in national publications including USA Today, Globe & Mail, Suspense Magazine, Publisher's Weekly, Oprah Mag, and First for Women.

K.A. Tucker currently resides outside of Toronto.
Learn more about K.A. Tucker and her books at katuckerbooks.com